Stone

Shadows

The Nephilim Chronicles II

Kenneth Davidson

1

Books by Kenneth Davidson

Modern Day Parables
Shinning Blackness

Copyright © 2013 by Kenneth Davidson
ISBN 13:978-0615876870
ISBN -10:0615876870
Cover photo provided by Shuttlestock © Capture Light

As unbiased as I can be, I declare this book by Kenneth Davidson as awesome and rate it Five Stars! However, it did ruin my chances of reading anything non-fictional for a while. It was such an engrossing saga that it has also impeded my own thriller-action writings...I find that I am inclined to insert too much of his thoughts into mine. The strength of the book is the author's ability to generate a thriller-action story based upon Biblical truths. Several surprising twists throughout the book, so the reader must be careful and the ending really got me! I loved that. Check it out. You can find Ken on Facebook and...Nephilim are real!

Patrick Richardson

Foreword

My parents moved to Scott County Tennessee when I was in the 6th grade and even though I had deep family roots in Scott County, I didn't seem to "fit in". I was bullied terribly, to the point that an older girl attacked me and hurt me physically. The physical pain was nothing compared to the mental anguish this experience caused me. I had been liked and loved my whole life up until then and was bewildered as to why someone wanted to cause me harm. That experience not only affected my confidence, but it caused me to question and doubt who I was as a person. It was at this time that I started studying martial arts. My teacher at the time was a college student home for the summer break. When it was time for him to go back to school, he introduced me to Kenneth and Paula Davidson, who agreed to continue teaching me martial arts. They were young, just out of college. They were serious, intense, but fun. Through their training they helped me build upon the foundation of the character traits that my family had already instilled in me....compassion, integrity, morals, and strength. We have remained friends through the years and I was honored when Kenneth asked me to assist with the editing of this book and write the foreword.

Kenneth's first book in "The Nephilim Series" was "Shining Blackness". The Nephilim, were the "sons of God" and the daughters of men" according to Genesis 6:4. In this first book, Kenneth begins the story of how these beings lived and interacted with humans through the years. At the end of the book, he leaves the reader wanting to know "what happens next..." In "Stone Shadows", his second book in the series, he continues the story and explores the human frailties that, we all struggle with, lust, greed, pride, envy etc. Although fictional in nature, there are some surprising truths throughout the storyline. The premise of this series is basically, good versus evil and how one can triumph over the other. This book "hooked" me right away and did not disappoint me. I can't wait to read the next one......to see what happens next.

Michelle "Shelly" Trammell Canada

4

This book is dedicated to Paula Davidson, my best friend, number one fan and wife of forty-four years.

Chapter 1

Frigged Lies from the Lips of a Hunter

"As snow in summer, and as rain in harvest, so
honor is not seemly for a fool."
Proverbs 26:1

Inaudible to human ears, the silk-lined scabbard releases its grip on the sword. The ancient weapon catches a flicker of sunlight filtering through the foliage of a massive white oak and glistens from a reflection of light. Small white cords securing its scabbard to the saddle bag sway softly in the gentle breeze of the early morning hours. They seem to be searching for seats in a large coliseum that will be advantageous in watching the battle that is soon to transpire.

The old sword slowly slices through the air coming to rest in a ready position above the soldier wielding it. Gingerly, he flexes his knees in preparation for battle with the hunter standing before him. The hunter poses with hands resting on hips ignoring the soldier who wields the sword. The soldier is confident the hunter has not detected his approach. Slow, stealth-like movements bring the soldier nearer the object of his focus. His plan is to quickly decapitate the hunter. He chuckles with delight that it will be achieved with the hunter's sword. The soldier is unaware that the creature standing before him is not human.

The hunter watches as small flames of fire begin to spread among slivers of wood which support larger pieces stacked atop them by the hunter. Soon, they will burn collectively, surge upward and consume the old farm house. It is the creature's way of parting from the past in search of a tomorrow in a land far from this God-forsaken country.

Every step the soldier takes is etched into the creature's mind; a perception of instinctive survival. Unknown to the approaching soldier, his attack will not surprise the hunter.

The soldier leaps forward quickly. His muscular frame enables him to cover the distance with one bound and his blade slices from right to left arching in an orbital path inches above and parallel to the shoulders of his adversary. Only the swish of the blade can be heard as it arches with such force that the soldier turns completely in the air, lands on his back in the dew soaked grass; yet, rolls instantly to his feet.

The charge consumes only seconds, but to his surprise the creature is faster. Not only does the hunter evade the sharp cold steel of the stolen blade, but now is nowhere in sight.

Years of combat training will not be wasted today. The soldier squats deep in a martial arts stance, learned many years ago, in an effort to equally distribute his weight. From this position, he can quickly move in any direction from which the anticipated counter-attack may come. His eyes shift from right to left as he rotates in a complete circle scanning the area. A gentle sway of a limb in the oak tree above warns him of danger. Instantly, he shifts his eyes upward in anticipation of an onslaught. It does not come. However, perching on a limb out of reach, the hunter glares down at him with a hellish smirk. Leisurely, a smile forms as lips open to speak.

"Well, Davy Boy, what took you so long? I've been waiting on you!"

Chapter 2

A Closet of Memories

"As the bird by wandering, as the swallow by
flying, so the curse causeless shall not come."
Proverbs 26:2

Tossing it carelessly on the bed, Beth unzips the large duffle bag.
She roughly flips it upside down dumping the contents atop the
smooth flowery bedspread.

"Wow," she says aloud, "what a great plan Alexander came
up with!"

She called him immediately after the fight in the Garden
and without hesitation he told her what to do. He was on his way
back from New York and would arrive by early evening, but she
would have everything he assigned completed prior to his arrival
from Reno.

The duffle contains Rosie's clothing which she removed
this morning after Rosie drifted into sleep at Beth and Phillip's
home. The missing clothes had convinced John Calvin that Rosie
had left him and returned to Riley. Now, Beth had to get the
clothes back and remove the Preacher's. When Rosie awakens
from the drug laced coffee, Beth will bring her home and convince

her that it was John Calvin that had abandoned her. She had to be quick and replace the clothing exactly as she found them. Women noticed their clothing, and how they stored them, much more than men. Besides, Alexander would not permit her to err.

Beth yanks the top drawer open in preparation to restore the clothes. This drawer had contained the panties which Beth now retrieves from the bed. First, the pink ones followed by the white, and then the others until all are placed in their proper locations. She places them exactly as she had removed them with lightning speed. If time permitted, she could actually replicate every fold and wrinkle in each garment. But that was beyond human perception; thus, not necessary today. After the panties, she folds bras to the center with socks and stockings to the right.

The second drawer is filled with jeans and slacks folded again as Rosie had stored them earlier. Philip's wife races to the closet to hang the last of the garments. Extraordinary human strength is employed by her fingers to iron out the creases she had caused from her cramped packing in the duffle. Beth sighs with pleasure enjoying the benefits of long life and energy acquired by being the mate of a Nephilim. Still, there is no time for gloating. She grabs the duffle bag from the bed and stuffs most of John Calvin's remaining clothes into it, along with a few of his personal items. She zips it with a quick yank of her hand. Beth watched the Preacher pull out a few minutes ago from the gas station in Kara's Ferrari before she returned to finish this assignment. The whole town knew he headed to Reno to retrieve his Harley.

Afterwards he would begin a northern route cross country to Tennessee.

Once again, a sigh escapes her lips. She looks around one last time to be sure all has been taken care of it. It has! The plan will now move into what she has titled as Phase 2. Unknown by the Preacher, the plan of escape given to him by Kara was the one Alexander had instructed her to give. The group assigned to follow him would gather valuable information to be forwarded to the Clan Leader.

Turning to make her exit, she inhales slowly and deeply. Her nostrils flare wide from the smell of desert flowers half a mile away. Raising her fist to the sky, she says softly, "I am the wife of Nephilim!" Exiting the parsonage, she remembers that her actions in public must be observed as normal.

Carelessly, she laughs aloud with excitement. She knows her role in the events soon to unfold in Cooper Town is valued by the Nephilim. Those events will initialize here, but spread through the whole country like an epidemic. It will grow until it proliferates in to a global movement. Within weeks, if all goes well, the very social, financial and political structure of the planet will be altered. The Nephilim Reformation is near and she too, will be a joint heir to worldly spoils and riches.

Chapter 3

The Awakening

"A whip for the horse, a bridle for the ass, and a
rod for the fool's back."
Proverbs 26:3

Light filters through the opening slits of her eyes. She strains to
open them completely, but the blinding light seeking to overcome
the blackness behind her eyelids is banned by the forcefulness of
her muscles closing them tightly again. A thousand thoughts race
through her mind like a large wheel spinning round and round in a
game show. Finally, she feels the muscles of her eyelids strain to
open her eyes. Through the small slits of the openings, she expects
a view of her bedroom. But, it is not to be! The scene is foreign;
thus, in confusion and frustration she closes her eyes again. There
is a futile attempt of raising her hands to rub her eyes as if she can
erase all the things that were not as they should have been.

"Where am I?" she asks the walls, finally able to open her
eyes completely.

Sitting in front of her is a strange woman. At first, she is
startled but then recognizes her as Beth.

"Good morning Sleepy Head!" chirps Beth. "And how are you feeling?"

"I'm fine," Rosie replies. "What happened?"

"My dear, you just slipped into sleep as we were having coffee this morning. I took the cup from your hand before you spilled it in your lap. You seemed to be so tired and resting so sweetly, that I could do nothing but tuck a pillow behind your head and let you sleep."

"Oh, I feel like I have…" Rosie pauses for a second. She wants to say she feels as though she has been drugged, but a small voice deep within her subconscious mind warns her to stay clear of those words.

"I feel like I have been asleep for years."

"Do you still want to drive to Carson City to shop today?" Beth asks. She gets the answer she both desires and expects.

"No, Beth. I don't. I'm really tired and would like to get back home and spend the day with Calvin. I may be coming down with a summer cold for I sure do feel weak."

"Okay darling. I'll drive you back. No need going if you don't feel like having a good time. Let me get my keys."

Rosie takes a deep breath and watches as Beth gets up and moves into the kitchen to retrieve her keys. There is something amiss here and Rosie cannot clear the cob webs from her head to pinpoint the problem. Nonetheless, for the first time since her arrival in Copper Town, Rosie feels that Beth is not to be trusted. The cordial atmosphere of their new friendship has dissipated.

From this moment forth, she decides to move with caution while in her presence, carefully choosing her words.

Rosie is somewhat wobbly, but refuses assistance as the two of them make their way to Beth's car. Neither of the women speaks a word until they arrive at the bottom of the stairs leading up to the parsonage.

"Are you going to be okay sweetie? You want me to come up and sit with you for a while?

"No, if I need anything I'll call you. John Calvin will take care of me."

With a growing sense of uneasiness, she is anxious to see her husband. It is he, and he alone, who can calm her and reassure her that everything is going to be okay.

Rosie closes the passenger door and begins the trek upward along the staircase. Today there seems to be a hundred steps and it takes every fiber of her being to climb each one. She pulls on the hand rail with her arms and lifts her long legs one at a time until she reaches the landing.

Before entering, she turns to watch Beth wave while circling the parking lot in her car. Beth waves again before driving onto 3rd Street and disappearing behind the building.

Across the street, Antonio waves at her. She thinks it odd that his perpetual smile is missing; nevertheless, she returns his wave and watches as he abruptly turns and heads for the Crematory she and Calvin nicknamed the "Rock".

"That's strange!" Rosie whispers aloud as she turns and stumbles to enter the parsonage.

In her car Beth laughs aloud with contempt before accelerating onto Main Street. She is eager to get home and await further instructions. She glances in the rear view mirror and is startled to see Rosie watching her from the balcony…she shivers from the sight. Regaining her composure, she mentally gives Rosie advice as if she were sitting beside her.

"Oh yes, my naïve and gullible little Rosie, we will talk again…real soon!"

Chapter 4

Rush of the Fool

"Answer not a fool according to his folly, lest
thou also be like unto him."
Proverbs 26:4

Hideous laughter reverberates in the farm yard sending chills
which dance along the soldier's spine. He has certainly
underestimated this creature. Nevertheless, fear is not part of his
nature and he has no plans to engage in frivolous conversation; a
fight he came for and a fight he will have. Revenge is his motive.

"Cat got your tongue, Davy Boy?"

Hunter shifts in the tree above him from one foot to the
other while clawing the air like a cat. It reminds Dave of a rabid
beast. Yet, he knows the Hunter is calculating a series of moves to
be utilized in an effort to destroy the human standing below.

"The sword your daddy stole from Alexander does not
glow in your hands Davy Boy! How can you expect to battle my
father and the leader of his clan without the power of the sword?

Today your ashes will join John Calvin's in the gray bag sitting by his Harley."

Dave knows of no clan or of a leader named Alexander. His name was John David McGarney, the son of John Calvin McGarney. His parents called him Dave when he was young, but only his mother was permitted to call him Davy. How dare this beast, perched like a baboon above him, use that name! He is more determined than before to thrust the beast to the hilt of the sharp sword.

The creature's alluding to the bag by the Harley containing ashes of his father registers in the depths of his mind and for a brief second, his concentration is interrupted. Imprudently, he allows his eyes to drift to the motorcycle in search of the gray bag. The cycle he recognized as the one he and his mother Rosie, had gotten his father a few years ago as a Christmas gift. His search is rewarded when he discovers a sack tied atop the saddle bag nearest him. John Calvin's Harley had been the goal of his approach from the wooded area behind the farm house. In the early morning darkness, he had carefully worked his way through the dangerous river gorge. His decision to do so without lights aided his undetected arrival.

Dave's thoughts are diverted for only seconds, but the hesitation serves as an initiative for a counter attack from the hunter balanced in the tree. Confident that the attack will catch the human off guard, the fiend leaps toward him with right foot landing first. The stride is not broken and as the left foot steps forward, a fist of iron smashes against Dave's right cheek. The hunter laughs, for a decision has been made to toy with the soldier as a cat would play with a mouse before devouring it. A lightning quick recovery by the soldier was not expected by the creature, even though the violent punch had sent him reeling backward knocking over the motorcycle. Dave's breathing is not hampered nor is his senses shaken. He rolls to his feet offering his attacker a laugh mockingly similar to the one the creature had given to Dave earlier. The creature turns to race to a rake near the fire. Grabbing it firmly in both hands, the wooden handle snaps below its metallic fixture.

Squaring up to Dave, the creature twirls the staff-like baton with such speed that it has the appearance of a helicopter blade. Laughter issues from the creature's throat, but ceases immediately when it observes blood dripping from Dave's sword.

The swirling staff ceases also. With a glance downward, the creature discovers the source of the crimson stain on Dave's sword. The creature's leather jacket is slit open from the sharp weapon displaying rock hard abdominal muscles, which have suffered the same fate as the jacket. Never has the creature encountered a human with such lightning quickness. With a loud snap, the dull end of the staff is slammed into the creature's arm pit with the sharp broken point extending toward the soldier. Then a thrust flows from the rear and upward as if striking the groin of an imaginary opponent. Like a shadow boxer, the creature performs several threatening moves with the staff that reveal the targets of the ensuing attack.

Dave is not impressed with the twirling threats for he has seen them many times.

Looking once again at the wound, the creature maintains a pose of defiance while indicating there will be no surrender due to a seemingly trivial injury. Turning abruptly and with ease, the beast leaps to the roof of the farm house. With a glance over the left shoulder, the creature's smirk evolves into a look of admiration and compassion for the human who will soon die.

This has no effect on Dave. His hatred for this creature is growing intensely; fueled by the realization that his father died at the hands of this evil beast.

With yet another laugh Dave's enemy disappears over the roof top.

Dave swears he will not be surprised again. He readies his sword and lowers his stance thinking the beast will never retreat. Soon it will appear (whether from his left, his right, or over the roof top he does not know) but he is prepared. Fixing his eyes on the center of the old farm house he allows his peripheral vision to take in all three possible avenues of the forthcoming attack. Since he was last seen by the creature with his sword in an upward position, he will wager his life the Hunter's next attack will come low.

He is correct. Sprinting from his left and appearing as a blur of light, a beast known by mankind as half-human and half-vampire, charges him. The point of its lance rips Dave's shirt and nicks his upper torso beneath his right arm. But, not before his upward thrust with the sword slices the rake handle into two near equal shafts. One is still grasped in the right hand of the creature while the other soars upward, spinning wildly in the air. He has completed his defensive move and steps backward to swing the blade again, but the beast shifts away to snatch the other piece of the rake in midair. With a high flying leap the creature returns. The two combatants stand only feet apart.

Squaring off, the creature begins spinning the new weapons in large figure eight circles that seem to completely protect the body of the beast. The circles increase with intensity and speed until the weapons are almost invisible. Dave is unable to see them at all for they are only blurs. Again, he is reminded of helicopter blades, perhaps because he rode them often during his career as a soldier. He focuses on the center of the creature's body as it circles him waiting for the opportune time to attack.

Once again, Dave is taken by surprise. While circling the fallen bike, the creature springs upward and over it. Dave expected the surge to come after clearing the bike. Only seconds transpire, but Dave has been hit repeatedly by the swirling sticks of the broken rake handle. His nose is bleeding and his upper lip is split. Knots swell on his head and his collar bone is bruised. The two warriors are tangled like two tom cats. Yet, it is human and half-human blood that mingles with the dew on the damp morning grass. As suddenly as it started, the fighting is over. Dave rolls into a sitting position with the creature lying across his lap with its head cradled in his left arm.

His gaze sinks deep into the bright emerald eyes of the creature. Small flecks of gold sparkle in an ocean of green and the whites of its eyes are as brilliant as snow. He sees the crimson flow oozing from the corner of the beast's mouth while observing the soft swollen lips. Swollen not from bruising, but a natural characteristic that humans admire and some emulate through medical and cosmetic alterations. For some reason, he desires to press those lips against his, but the squeaky whisper of the creature's voice breaks his hypnotic lust. The left hand of the creature slowly finds Dave's right hand and squeezes it tightly. Dave cannot free his hand from the strong grip of the creature for he holds the handle of his sword; a sword that has passed through the creature and penetrated to the hilt. The tip is buried into the ground behind the creature. Blood flows down the length of it. This beast will soon pass from life to death. The soldier cannot stop; he brushes the long flowing auburn hair from its face.

"So you desire to kiss the lips you so hate my little Davy?" the beast laughs derisively. "Come closer Davy Baby and let me tell you a secret."

Dave places his lips close to those of the beast and turns his ear to listen to the dying words of this creature who slew his father.

The Hunter laughs hideously and begins to speak the last words of life.

"What's the matter Davy boy? Can you not face the passion that rages inside you? Do you not know that my father will rip the heart from your dying carcass and drink your blood like wine, even though you are my little brother?"

The laughter comes again, somewhat softer.

"My father took your mother when she was a young girl, just before she and John Calvin were married. You never knew…did you?"

"The strength you have comes from the blood of the Nephilim that created you my little brother. And the one that made you will also slay you for he knows that you are neither Maseth nor Bachar."

Dave's anger rekindles. He slowly pulls the sword out several inches and gazing down once more into the emerald pools, he plunges it hard and watches as the white of Hunter's eyes cloud and life departs.

"Remember this day, little brother. Just remember when death faces you too, that you took the life of your sister. You are as I am. You too, little brother, are Banah!"

Chapter 5

Purple and Scarlet

"Answer a fool according to his folly, lest he be
wise in his own conceit."
Proverbs 26:5

Alexander stretches his legs, leisurely reclining in the oversized chair of his Dassault Falcon 7X knowing that once they were airborne, his pilot will cruise at the maximum speed of Mach 90.

Top priority from the control tower for departure was never a challenge, nor was it today. That, the pilot confesses, could only be achieved by Alexander. Within hours, he will entertain the same privilege in Reno; even if commercial flights are to be interrupted.

The clan leader's private jet was custom manufactured to accommodate the Nephilim in both: their human and created forms. Four large seats, nearly twice the size of regular ones, were arranged diagonally through the cabin with four regular sized seats adjacent to them. A zigzag pattern resulted for the aisle. This arrangement offered two individual conference-type seating areas; an arrangement conducive for his flights throughout the world with those of his kind and the humans who were part of his organization.

Philip swivels his seat to face the Council Chairman while leaning backwards to stretch. He fills the seat while watching as Alexander also slowly assumes his Nephilim form. Respectfully, he waits for him to initiate the conversation. The two human employees settle down for the return trip to Copper Town; today, they will not employ conversation unless called upon by one of the two Nephilim.

"Well, it did not go exactly as we planned my old friend," begins the leader.

"That's true but I feel that Beth's report is accurate," answers Philip in defense of his wife.

Alexander sighs. His ancient life has brought him much pleasure – and many disappointments. At this particular moment, a conglomerate of both entangles the fiber of his soul.

"I know." he replies. "I wish Michael had stayed out of it. His death was not planned. All the others were expendable, but it will take a lot of work to restructure now that my son is gone."

"Look on the bright side my old comrade; your daughter will survive until you arrive to heal her. Today you came close to losing two of your most devoted children."

"Yes, I would have missed her as well if she had been killed. Sometimes I wonder if I can trust that girl! There is too much of her mother's blood flowing through her veins. Above and beyond that, she can be reckless at times."

"She'll be okay. Kara is a Gionni; shrewd and committed to our cause. She takes after you."

Philip pauses before giving his best interpretation of a human laugh and then adds, "Kara will do precisely as you say."

"Or endure the disparaging hand of her father," he replies. "Come let us discuss the changes we will make when we get back to Copper Town."

Both return their seats to an upright position for rest is not a necessity for the Nephilim. They sleep if they desire; nevertheless there is no stipulation or luxury in either. When choosing the option to sleep, their minds are completely aware of their surroundings.

With favorable winds wrought by the hands of the Nephilim, the trip will be swift. When they land in Reno, all restructuring of the Nephilim world empire will be ready for immediate implementation.

Chapter 6

Streets of Music

"He that sendeth a message by the hand of a fool
cutteth off the feet, and drinketh damage."
Proverbs 26:6

Music City roars with the sound of a Thunder Mountain Custom Spitfire speeding along I-40 westward to Memphis. Zigzagging through lunch hour traffic, it exercises maneuvers that carry the rider past one vehicle after another. Long lines of semis and automobiles are conquered as the Spitfire races towards a nonexistent finish line. At times, it passes on the shoulder. Other times, it roars atop the broken white lines separating the lanes and bringing the rider within inches of automobiles to his left and right.

This particular pro-street bike had been customized by Lisa. Not only did she design spectacular cycles, she also fabricated them. Lisa was a dear friend and she was one of the few women he had ever come to trust. He admired her greatly for she was not the typical weak and whining female.

For his bike, she designed a drop-seat that seemed to surge into one of a kind saddle bags. Only a woman would envision such a spectacular pattern. Their tear drop shape complimented the contours of the bike's ample frame. They swung upward in the rear accenting a screaming eagle muffler system before fading into large compartments behind and just below the rider's buttocks. She hand stitched the soft leather meticulously. The same care was taken when she attentively attached silver studs along the leather seams of the seat and saddle bags exactly as he requested.

In spite of Lisa's demanding schedule at her Fayetteville shop, she completed John David's bike in record time. Although it was offered as a gift to him, Dave refused the generosity and tipped her considerably more than the prearranged price. The pleasure she afforded would not be taken advantage of. If she had time for vacation, she would be riding behind him now on this adventure.

Thoughts of Lisa fade as the big Harley engine responds to the generosity of Dave's open throttle.

Careening between two semis, Dave watches the driver on the right threaten him with a move towards the center line. There are only inches between him and the large truck to his left. Quickly, he wrenches on the throttle and the bike rockets forward. Entering the right lane ahead of the big rig, he eases a large steel ball bearing from his jacket pocket with his left hand. He has mastered this art and will once again find it rewarding. With his thumb, as a child would cast a marble, he flips the bearing over his left shoulder. In his rearview mirror, he watches in anticipation as the ball bearing searches for its target. It soars upward like a homing pigeon and comes to rest on the trucker's large windshield, inches from the driver's face. Although Dave cannot hear the engine brakes echo, he knows they are applied by the driver for he watches the truck weave a little, slow and move towards the outside shoulder. This is Dave's prompt to move ahead hurriedly. The bike crosses to the right lane shoulder passing a van and then crosses three lanes of traffic in its search for the far left lane barely in time to make the intersection of I-40 west where it separates from I-65 north. Within seconds, the newly cracked windshield and the truck to which it is attached are left behind, never to be seen by Dave again.

To his right, he sees the Broadway Street Exit. The sign brings to mind his last trip to Nashville a few years ago. He was home in Riley on leave and decided to depart the boring rural life to grasp the excitement of night-life in the capitol of country music. The first night there he met an electric fiddle player at Tootsie's Orchid Lounge. She was a beautiful woman with long brown hair and eyes that matched. He was immediately fascinated with her as she moved along the narrow bar alternating from the corner stage with her band to the crowded street with the cordless fiddle. When their eyes met, they both knew that at closing time they would leave together. A late night meal was enjoyed before they spent the remainder of the night enjoying each other…until the sun came up.

He shakes his head and moves through slowing traffic. Yes, a lot of things happened in only a few days from their first meeting. He spent the next evening with her at the world renowned Lounge, known by most simply as Mom's, and afterwards the first night activities was duplicated. Both were in need of sleep, but neither entertained the thought of rest…forsaking all for pleasure. When nightfall came, they were off for a few hours of dancing and drinking at the Wild Horse Saloon. They worked up a sweat in the old remodeled three story historic warehouse before leaving on the General Jackson Showboat. Traveling along the river they had their first decent meal accompanied with more of their favorite brew. And then, disaster struck.

He later told police that while they stood embraced along the rear rail, a scuffle broke out inside the Showboat. Opening the doors to investigate the source of the ruckus, more from curiosity than a desire to assist, he watched as security broke up a fight and escorted the brawlers away. When he returned to the fiddle player, she was gone. At the very moment he prepared to move about the boat to look for her, he heard her screaming. Another couple standing near the rail pointed toward the ever increasing gulf between the boat and her thrashing body.

He spent several days in Nashville undergoing grueling questioning by Nashville Metro Police. Yet, it took only hours for him to be cleared when C.I.A. officials appeared. Although his leave had been shortened, he was cleared of any criminal charges as the death had been ruled accidental.

"No" he said as his words were choked by the wind in his teeth, "although I am a patient man....I will spend no time in Nashville tonight."

Callously, he dismisses the thoughts of the young lady, and her music, from his memories. And as they fade, so do the city limits of Music City.

Chapter 7

Bottled Tears

"The legs of the lame are not equal: so is a parable
in the mouth of fools."
Proverbs 26:7

"John Calvin!" She yells while moving with a steady pace down the hallway of the parsonage. It was the title used when she was upset with him, or in dire need of his companionship. If her preacher man was there, he would know it to be the latter.

"Calvin?" She calls again. Her question concerns his whereabouts more than a desire for conversation. Rosie rushes into the living room, her eyes squinting in observation of the little table next to the sofa. Her husband never left home without his Bible and if he left voluntarily, it would not be there. Her face bears witness that it is gone and thus, he must be out ministering! Joy flees when she realizes that their family picture is also unaccounted for. They had never been parted from the photo of them taken with John David when he was only a baby. It was their first, and most cherished, family photo. She refuses to speculate about the reason for its absence.

Hurriedly, Rosie rushes to the bedroom and scrutinizes the bed she made fresh a few hours ago before walking to Beth's house. Atop the smooth spread is a plastic container which usually contained Calvin's riding gear. Facing her, the empty box divulges evidence she does not desire, but cannot be denied. On the crest of the pillow, a lid rests, hastily thrown aside. It will never be known by her, that Beth masterfully arranged it after returning Rosie's clothes - only minutes ago. Little was known about the Preacher and his wife; however, local people were aware of their lives being manipulated by the Nephilim.

Rushing to the doors of the closet, she yanks them open only to discover it partially emptied. The Preacher's dress clothes still hang neatly beside hers, but his casual clothes are gone. Whirling, she urgently moves to the chest of drawers. First, she yanks open the top drawer which contains his underwear. The drawer is empty! She slams it shut and spontaneously jerks the second one open that contains his socks and tee shirts. It too is empty!

A sickening feeling overtakes her as she recalls the words of her husband explaining a desire, and need, for them to leave this place. Perhaps her argument supporting their unfinished work had not been convincing. Without warning, she feels abandonment. Her shoulders sag; unable to support the heaviness of her wilting head. Inhaling with a slow, deep breath, she releases it like a typhoon. A second deep breath is released while she yells to the walls with her fists clinched tightly in defiance.

"No! No! No! I know he would never leave me alone here!"

Her thoughts go back to the look on Beth's face when she awoke on her couch moments ago. She does not understand fully, yet, what Beth knows, but Rosie is convinced she is hiding something.

"I don't trust her," she continues in the conversation with the walls. "I know she drugged me this morning for some reason...I know she did."

She vows in her heart to never trust that woman again. Further, Rosie pledges to carefully choose her words while around Beth and Philip from this day forward. Her sworn declaration of anger fades to feelings of loneliness. For the first time in Rosie's life she feels there is no one to turn to, no one to call on...no one to trust.

The plastic container is sent smashing into the nearest wall where it is immediately joined by the lid. Overwhelming emotions of confusion encompass her body. She collapses face first into the pillow of her beloved husband.

"Where are you John, what's happened to you?"

She cries and pulls the pillow into her face while curling slowly into a fetal position.

"Where are you?" She asks again.

She detects the scent of her husband's body deep within his pillow as she breathes through it. It is a weak substitute, but it becomes her much needed companion. She squeezes it tightly in remembrance of their life-long journey together.

Rosie does not know she will never see her husband again, but she realizes that Beth is the only one she can talk with on this island of desolation…the only one who might be able to give her a clue as to what happened to John Calvin. She will have to call her, but for the moment she tightly holds the pillow. It is soaked with the dampness of tears as her weeping turns into uncontrollable sobs of sorrow. Her crying results in total exhaustion which serves to console her as she drifts into sleep.

Chapter 8

The Return of the Council

"As he that bindeth a stone in a sling, so is he that giveth honor to a fool."
Proverbs 26:8

Fluttering to the right and back to the left, the Falcon 7X wobbles; yet, is determined to make contact with the runway at Reno International Airport. Thermals drifting over the Sierra Mountains from the west combined with perpetual winds from the desert below will provide anything but a welcome for the Falcon. Rarely did he land the Clan Leader's jet without some turbulence in this city. With no reluctance, the plane approaches slightly sideways. As one wheel touches the asphalt, the pilot easily drops the upwind wing to straighten the plane's landing. To those on board, it was a great landing; to the pilot it was simply what he and other pilots were trained to do.

Within seconds, he brings the jet into the return lane to taxi to the private hanger of Alexander. The architectural structure of the leader's hanger is taller than others surrounding it. The building contains an office and conference room. Both display large twenty foot walls complete with proportional furniture; correct decor for Nephilim in their created forms. Seldom, did clan members use the suite. Its use would not be employed today either.

With the Falcon yet rolling, Alexander moves to the door. As soon as the thrusters are shut down he hears the ground crew moving swiftly outside to place the steps used for exiting. In spite of a desire to leap to the pavement, Alexander remembers he is in the eyes of the public. Such action is forbidden, but soon he will no longer have to hide behind the weak human form he inhabited. His ground crew works feverishly to get the steps in place at the very moment the plane comes to rest. Promptly, they open the door and move away humbly to allow the leader to descend unimpeded. Alexander is the first to exit and with only a few bags in his hands he heads directly to his Bell 407 helicopter. The engine hums readily with a new pilot ready to assume his leg of the grueling relay trek.

By automobile (unless Alexander's daughter was driving) it is a three hour drive from Reno to Copper Town. The Bell's Rolls Royce 250-C47B turbine will soon reach its maximum speed of 160 miles per hour and with a strong prevailing tail wind, the pilot will cover the 173 mile flight in less than an hour.

Philip follows in the footsteps of his leader. The two human employees sprint to catch up with the Nephilim. Their attempts are futile and they know a severe chastising will follow for their failure. They will be left behind today if they do not hurry. The ground crew continues to perform their assignments; all fearfully avoid the eyes of the Nephilim. They simply answer yea for yea and nay for nay if questions are asked. Today, there are no such questions or comments.

Alexander remembers a time long ago when Egyptian workers responded in the same manner when he visited the work sites of the Great Pyramids. He cackles a laugh no one can understand, and no one dares ask, remembering a television documentary he watched years ago. During the program, the producer gave his hypothesis on the methods that might have been used to construct them. Nevertheless, in the end they surmised that no one knew how the massive stones had been moved into position.

He laughed the same laugh then and thought, *I can tell you for I supervised the construction of them all; however, some things are left best unknown.*

Philip laughs for he knows what Alexander is thinking. He pats him on the back while moving into the spacious cabin. The Bell was normally designed for five passengers with wide-open, spacious seating. This one was redesigned to Alexander's specifications. He had it overcrowded with two oversized chairs and two smaller ones.

The men climb aboard as the helicopter lifts from the ground before the doors can be closed. Today their delay will not be lengthy for the Clan Leader's aircraft moves across the runway and climbs rapidly above the mountains to the east.

Fifteen miles out, the pilot looks down on the famous Mustang Ranch and smiles. He spent the whole night, and a large chunk of money, at that ranch. It had been well spent for he had thoroughly enjoyed the ride on the mustang mare he rented.

Alexander slaps him on the back and laughs. The helicopter pilot learned many years ago that Alexander can read all of his thoughts.

Chapter 9

Saddle Scared

"As a thorn goeth up into the hand of a drunkard,
so is a parable in the mouth of fools."
Proverbs 26:9

The little dove gives her best effort to escape the predator racing below. Her flight is strong and fast but soon she gives in to exhaustion; her struggles are no match for the cycle she thinks is chasing her. The bike races westward along I-40 and within seconds leaves the little bird abandoned to continue her trip to a favorite roosting site. If able to discern the thoughts of a human mind, she would have been saddened by the thoughts swirling within Dave's mind. She would have discovered the loneliness and despair that overshadowed him. Throughout most of his life, Dave sensed he had been deserted. It was a desertion that caused him to repeatedly sink into a deep sea of depression where there was no escape. His never-ending crusade to find some form of prolonged happiness only left him emptier than when he first began. Pleasures of this world soothed his aching heart for short periods of time, but afterwards he sank again into the murk of solitude.

Female companionship was a favorite escape, yet it was never satisfying or lasting. Many a morning he awoke to find the light of day shining down on a woman he had picked up during the night. Most of the time, the sight of his female companion sickened him. Thus, they were dismissed quickly with brusque words. Although they gave him pleasure, he had no time or patience for cheap and frivolous pillow talk. He was never gentle in telling them that upon his return, he expected them to be gone. To him, women were nothing but objects, or toys, and should be discarded like trash afterwards. He found them to be easily seduced; believing the simplest of lies while seeking to change all men they meet into what they perceived men should be. They meet men in bars and the next week they want them to attend some little funky family church. An encounter with him was rarely anything beyond a one night stand.

Dave was not his father's son. He followed his parents, no choice of his own, from one missionary field to another. Never was he able to settle down and have any type of lasting friendship. Perhaps, he often conjectured, that is the reason for his screwed-up outlook on life.

Lisa was different. He wishes she was riding with him now for it was going to be a long haul tonight. He had decided earlier to ride across Oklahoma before resting. Nearly a thousand miles separated Riley, Tennessee from Elk City, Oklahoma but he hopes to cover that distance by mid morning. The KOA campground in Elk City was a favorite stop of his. Once there, he would rest for a day before resuming his trip. He had to get some sleep; nevertheless, he knew traveling at night would be best on the first day of his journey.

Lisa and he had made several grueling rides together over the years. Their endurance outings were often referred to as "runs". They both joined the Iron Butt Association (IBA) of over 50,000 members and accomplished every award offered. Several times they rode 1000 miles in less than twenty-four hours to claim the Saddle Sore Award. And more than once, they rode the 1500 miles in less than 36 hours to claim the Bun Burner Certificate. Lisa, like Dave, had also achieved those awards while riding solo.

The long morning hours in Riley and the fight with Hunter were deciding factors causing him to favor the Saddle Sore tonight over the Bun Burner. He was an experienced endurance rider, but he was no fool. Besides, if he had gotten more rest, he would have ridden straight to Cooper Town. That would have been easier than his and Lisa's coast-to-cost ride under fifty hours. The IBA calls it the 50 CC. After spending a wild night in Myrtle Beach, with little sleep, they dipped their front wheels into the Atlantic Ocean and 45 hours later, they did the same in the Pacific.

"Yep," he thought, "the world is a playground…might as well eat, drink and be merry…for tomorrow we die!"

Chapter 10

A Time for Rest

"The great God that formed all things both rewardeth the fool, and rewardeth transgressors."
Proverbs 26:10

Blinding light is suddenly reflected in both rear view mirrors of Dave's bike. With his left hand, never letting up on the throttle with his right, he twists the left one down and then the right one. He knows the dangers of the setting sun, and in this case the rising sun, in his mirrors.

"I've made better time than I thought I would," he exclaims to the trees along the road side.

The day is just breaking and within an hour or so he will make the exit to the KOA between Clinton and Elk City, Oklahoma. The trip included 715 miles from Nashville ridden mostly by the headlight of his motorcycle and 180 miles from Riley to Nashville. All that in less than 20 hours; however he would not qualify for the Saddle Sore. He would be lacking 70 miles. It was not his objective, but rather an observation he made. Soon, he will pitch his pup tent on one of the grassy sites and take a short walk to Clinton Lake before showering and settling down for a few hours of sleep. Sometime tonight, he planned to eat at the RV dining room before reading the manuscript addressed to Alexander Gionni. He had taken everything Hunter had packed, excluding her clothes. When he had time, he would go through all the items to see what might be useful.

After arriving at the KOA site, it takes Dave only a few minutes to get his campsite rented. He straddles the bike and idles down the little lane to the isolated site he had chosen. For a second, he thinks of throwing the tent aside to merely sleep on the grass. With his sleeping bag atop the tent, he could awaken later to the light of the stars and the promising fullness of the moon. But trepidation of oversleeping combined with a desire for privacy fuels him with enough energy to complete the task of erecting the tent. Once completed, he crawls inside and immediately succumbs to the darkness of sleep.

Chapter 11

An Eastward Wind

"As a dog returneth to his vomit, so a fool
returneth to his folly."
Proverbs 26:11

As a tailwind fills the sails of a ship and sends it skipping upon the waves of its journey, a strong eastward wind blows from Reno towards Cooper Town. It tilts the powder coated Bell 407 slightly forward assisting the helicopter through the arid desert sky. The pilot chuckles audibly knowing his employer will be pleased with this record breaking flight. His imagination soars with the thought that Alexander, in some supernatural way, is directing the winds by a willful desire to expedite the trip.

One thing is for sure, he must be careful of his thoughts. Even now, since he cannot shake the memories of his visit to the Mustang Ranch, he knows they are being shared by at least two others; thus, not completely his own. He understands, to some degree, that Nephilim are able to read the minds of most humans. Especially, when they focus on one particular thought!

He remembers one of the long forgotten Bible lessons his grandmother taught him as a child. She instructed him not worry or dwell upon negative things since you could not change even the color of your hair by doing so. He wonders if that warning also could prevent supernatural beings from reading your mind.

A sinister growl from the throat of Alexander in the back seat warns him to get his mind where it belongs: the flight to Copper Town. Religion and Biblical conversations, and thoughts, were discouraged by Alexander. If you brought them to him, you best be prepared to know what you were talking about. He had personally heard the Clan leader quote verse after verse when debating with Bible scholars. The pilot was convinced that Alexander had the whole book memorized.

Forgetting the warning the fiendish growl, his thoughts return to the little lady he met last night at the brothel. He paid her top dollar, and tipped even more, in hopes for some private company. It was money well spent since they made plans to spend time together on her day off. Alexander's laugh assures him that, also, will cost him dearly.

"Good job Jim," praises the Nephilim leader as the helicopter dips from the North West towards the helipad at the rear of Alexander's casino.

Jim only laughs for he does not know if the Nephilim is complimenting him on his flying skills or his plans for the night.

"Take me directly home," he continues.

"We will pick up Kara and then you will bring me back to the casino."

Swiftly, Jim regains the lost altitude to fly over the casino. Looking down into the parking, he observes Beth, Phillip's wife, climbing the steps to the parsonage. She waves at Alexander. Jim does not hear the Nephilim leader mentally giving instructions to her.

Job well done Beth, he assures her telepathically.

Yes, he continues. *That is exactly what I want you to do! After I take care of Kara, I'll be back down to deal with my Shining Blackness...my sweet little Rosie.*

Chapter 12

The Journey of a Wayward Woman

"Seest thou a man wise in his own conceit? There
is more hope of a fool than of him."
Proverbs 26:12

*Your phone's ranging! Hey, your phone's ranging! YOUR
PHONE'S RANGING!*

She laughs; reaching out across the sheets to squeeze the
only companion she had last night - her cell phone. Honestly, the
ring tone annoyed her as much as others who heard it. But, there
was a great deal of pleasure for her to watch the disgust spread
across faces of those who heard it ring. For that reason alone, she
kept the phone on maximum volume to announce all her calls.

People, to her, were like mad rats in a maze. Running here
and there, they never seemed to be aware of anyone else's
existence but theirs. Her phone was one method she had of letting
them know the world did not revolve around their selfish and
greedy ways. In shopping malls, they stood around yakking and
blocking isles; defiantly refusing to move. She just burst through
the middle of those crowds with no apologies while daring them to

voice any opposition. Those that did were recipients of her vast vocabulary consisting of obscenities not publicly acceptable. To those that threatened violence, she quickly extended an invitation to meet her in the parking lot after shopping; females and males without any discrimination. Some along the course of her life had accepted the invitation, to their demise. She had silenced all challengers putting each down quickly and effortlessly.

"Hello Dad, how's it going?" she answers after viewing the caller ID.

"Fine Len!" the voice answers. "Listen, we have him located. He is in Oklahoma at a KOA campground. He's rented a tent site until tomorrow morning. Where are you?"

"I spent the night above Albuquerque last night and decided to sleep in."

"If you are with someone else, get rid of them and get on the road now!"

"No, Dad, I don't have company. I am alone. What do you want me to do?"

"The plan has not changed! I'm sending you the address along with some pictures of him. When you check in, our people will give you all the information you need."

"Okay, I can be on the road in about an hour. That should put me there by midafternoon."

"Great! Listen Orlenda, don't let me down. Do whatever you need to do and any way you want... just get it done. Do you understand?"

She loved it when he called her Orlenda. It was the name her Russian mother had chosen for her. It meant female eagle. Over the years, she had lived up to that name and was still living up to it. She was the instrument of prey her father personally trained her to be. His will was always placed first in her life and the constant effort to please him drove her relentlessly onward. The rewards for her faithful service were never short of her expectations. Her father lavished her with gifts and money beyond human comprehension. Obedience to him was not something to be toyed with, it was absolutely demanded. Her name was shortened to Len by family and friends even though she desired Orlenda. Hearing it from her father, who she worshipped, made it all the more desirable. What she desired more than anything was to hear her father say he loved her. The love he had for her was well perceived, but the words had never been voiced. Sometimes, she felt as if she was only a tool for him and his clan; nevertheless, she would carry out his wishes.

"Yeah, I understand Dad. Have I ever let you down?"

"No Orlenda, you have not. Just be careful. This is no ordinary man. He is a vicious and ruthless killer. But, he thinks no one knows. That is your advantage. Call me when the job is done and remember what I told you yesterday."

"I'll take care of it Dad."

"Okay, I'll talk to you when it is finished. If anything changes, I'll call you."

"Bye, Dad," she whispers into the phone.

Knowing she will not be answered, she manages the words, "I love you Dad." The click on the other end signifies she was heard, but the response she so longs for, once again, does not come.

"Oh well...." She says leaping from the bed of her motor home to stare at her naked body in the full length mirror. She twists from one pose to another watching the muscles ripple beneath her flawless milky white skin. She inherited those qualities from her mother along with the feminine perfection. She vowed often to work on a tan, but it seemed such a waste of time.

Observing the protrusion of her muscular buttocks, she laughs while gently slapping the right cheek and softly whispers, "I've never had a man complain about my skin!"

Not to be outdone, the twin in the mirror turns and tenderly rubs the other cheek. Shaking her head, Len examines her full frontal pose. Her eyes sweep quickly up her torso, scrutinizing her breasts before resting on her face. Greens eyes, inherited from her father and his people, glisten like emeralds. Her hair also was inherited from her father. It was thick, coarse as straw, and sprung forth from her scalp like exploding flames of a wild fire. It was naturally wavy and curved in several directions as the ends came to rest well beneath her shoulders.

She brushes it back and gathers it seductively in her hands. With her elbows held high and wide, she profiles her body again with an ever widening smile from the inspection of her breasts. It takes only a slight drop from raised toes to send them bouncing

51

pleasantly before her. She giggles, uncharacteristically, like a teenager.

"This is going to be exciting," she declares to the woman in the glass.

"Dad says this man has no regard for women and is a male chauvinist."

"Ha!" Her reflection declares, "A lot like you. Yes, I agree. This job will be pleasurable."

Len drops the hair knowing there is little time to waste. She must get her motor home disconnected and on the road again.

"A shower is a necessity," she again addresses the woman in the glass knowing that it will take most of the day for her hair to dry while traveling I-40 eastward. There was simply no time to dry it with a dryer which was her usual method. The hair was so thick, that if not dried thoroughly, it would mold. And even with the dryer, it took an hour to free it from all moisture.

With both hands, she gives her buttocks a double pat before vanishing behind the colorful stained glass doors of her shower.

Chapter 13

Granting Hope to a Fool

"The slothful man saith, there is a lion in the way;
a lion is in the streets."
Proverbs 26:13

"Need help young lady?" asks the old man who has quietly eased behind Len.

He does not know this beautiful young woman heard every step he made from the time he left the motor home next door to where he now stands close behind her.

"No thanks," She chirps turning slowly from her squatting pose to face him. She just finished storing the last of the hookups and has no time to chat with this old man. Clad only with short cut-off blue jeans, a man's shirt (purposely left unbuttoned and secured only with a quick tie at the tails), she bends over intentionally allowing a spillage of what the shirt should have contained.

I'll give this old man a little glance of what he came to see, she thinks, not rushing to restore the slippage.

The old man glances over his shoulder to see if the woman of his age is watching from the window of their coach…she is! He clears his throat and says sheepishly, "well, if you change your mind, I'll be around!"

Len laughs while thinking, *hummm…of course you will.* She watches him walk away with his head hanging low from the glare of his wife. His walk entices her and she concludes *he's not bad for an old geezer. If I had time I might just see what he is up to. He calls me young lady, but would he ever be amazed to know that I'm twice his age. Humans, I guess it's only fair they should age so quickly since they are so ignorant.*

"Thanks," she shouts out. "I'll keep that in mind!"

As she stands up, the old man shamefully makes his way back to his motor home under the piercing eyes of his wife. Len decides to fasten a few of the lower buttons. She spins, leaps into the cab and plops into the driver's seat. Hastily, she keys the ignition.

The 525 hp Cat C-13 diesel engine purrs as if more eager to leave than its driver. Her 40 foot motor coach was easy to steer in and out of tight places since it was just under the length restrictions of most car/trailer rigs. That allowed her to go places that others could not. Nevertheless, it was more luxurious than the average American home. This particular model, Intrigue, had been custom made for her by her father Alexander with no monetary concern or limitation.

"Whatever my daughter wants," had been his instructions to the manufacturer.

At night, she utilized the front and rear flood lights by remote control. The upgrades of all stainless steel fixtures with medium cherry cabinets matched all other woodwork throughout the unit. Additional storage had been designed for her bedroom to accommodate a vast wardrobe along with other miscellaneous supplies. The Pioneer GPS was seldom needed for she had driven through this country long before the interstate system was constructed. She knew the western regions of the nation better than the back of her hand.

Len did appreciate the Digital "In Motion" Satellite System since she enjoyed evenings watching TV. Reading was not to her liking, so she had made sure the coach was well supplied with a TV in the living room and another in the bedroom. But it was time for her to enjoy the ultra-soft leather driver's seat that matched the plushness of all her furniture. A rear door included in the design was barely noticeable. The "one of a kind" design consisted of a fold out ramp that served as an elevator/lift for the large upper storage room. If all went as planned, she would soon have a custom motorcycle stored in that area for the return trip.

Within seconds, the campground is left behind as she travels southward through Albuquerque. On the south side of the city, she merges onto I-40 East and sets the cruise control at 80 mph. The engine continues to purr upward out of the valley floor like a contented kitten finishing a warm bowl of milk. At this pace, she is assured of making it to the campgrounds by midafternoon at the latest. Her sources report that the man she is looking for has already checked in. With early arrival, he was charged for two days and confirmed he would be there until tomorrow morning. If that is the case, she will have plenty of time to spin her web of deception that will be his demise.

Len sits back after turning the stereo volume to maximum. The whole motor home seems to join in with her excitement. She bounces on the seat behind the steering wheel and allows her humming to grow increasingly louder. An eerie sound of the diesel engine fails in its attempt to harmonize with the music or the voice of the driver.

For a second, she thinks about watching for speed-traps but dismisses that quickly. She unbuttons her shirt again to the tie, laughing as it opens wide. One look at the pilot of this coach would be enough for most wandering eyes, with badges pinned to their chest, to forget any speeding citations. Those not impressed with the view would yield to her persuasive and hypnotic abilities.

Probably more of them yielded to her persuasion than to the view her blouse provided; although she imagined the latter. Occasionally, she had paid tickets to those not attracted to women and to those who were beyond the influence of her hypnosis.

Soon, her green eyes will stare into the eyes of the stranger she has been dispatched to destroy….John David McGarney.

Her words of harmony do not match the lyrics booming from the stereo, but she sings them nonetheless.

"You're no different than any other man," she sings. "Your lust will be your end."

Chapter 14

A Blanket of Blood

"As the door turneth upon his hinges, so doth the slothful upon his bed."
Proverbs 26:14

The helicopter lands smoothly on the lawn behind Alexander's vast mountain chalet. His home, exclusively constructed of walnut timbers, stands majestically overlooking the small capitol of the Nephilim Empire. Visitors to the tiny township of Copper Town, Nevada never suspect that it is the center of a large and complex world organization, nor that it will soon be the capitol of the world. If all goes as the Nephilim clans planned at their New York meeting, a new world-wide economic system would soon emerge. The very existence of humanity would depend upon their alliance with the new world leader, Alexander Gionni. And all of this was scheduled to fall into place within the next four weeks. Just in time for the Nephilim Feast Yiqqaha.

Jim keeps the engine running, watching as Alexander bails out and vanishes like a blurry streak across the lawn. Within seconds he reappears at the helicopter's entry with his daughter Kara in his arms. She is wrapped with an expensive blanket woven of silk, most of which is blood soaked. Kara is unconscious. Her breathing is shallow and her vital signs have dropped. The snap of Alexander's finger reverberates throughout the cabin like thunder. It is a signal to his pilot for a quick departure. For a brief time, the Nephilim leader is suspended in air as the helicopter lifts. His snapping finger is inside the cabin, but his feet have not completed the jump. Nevertheless, Jim lifts up and quickly obtains top speed. Within seconds, he sails downward to the little town at the foothills of the Toiyabe Mountain Range knowing that Alexander completed his leap.

"Drop me off at the roof portal!" Alexander commands.

"Yes sir!" is his answer.

Jim hovers over the area of the roof which he knows conceals the portal of a secret place of thunder that only the Nephilim and their invited guests are allowed to enter.

Alexander leaps from the helicopter in his human form with his half-human daughter clutched in his arms. Within the twinkling of an eye, his form changes in midair into his huge ancient form: the form of a Nephilim. Directly behind him follows Philip who also transforms into the dark cobalt colored giant of his Nephilim form. Both appear to be more animal than human as they disappear through the portal.

Jim lands the 407 at the helipad and shuts down all systems. He knows his services will not be needed again for a few days and has been given permission to make a quick departure for a long drive back to Reno. There, he will spend a few days with his new lady of the night. He smiles while making his exit and leaves the other two men to unload the cargo. Jim knows very little of the ways of the Nephilim and desires to know less. It's best that way he often reminds himself. Yet…thoughts deep within his mind tells him he might know more…if he had been allowed to remember.

Chapter 15

In the Hands of Raphah

"The slothful hideth his hand in his bosom; it
grieveth him to bring it again to his mouth."
Proverbs 26:15

Lush vegetation normally found only in tropical regions springs upward fourteen to sixteen feet to a light source brighter than the most brilliant man-made lights. The ultra violet rays find their way through the leaves to fall upon the freshened earth like floodlights in a theater. The earthly region contained within this interior garden above the Gionni Casino is as real as any contained without. Alexander lands upon the stony pathway running through the garden and moves along the diamond bright rock-way to the staircase leading down into the council chambers.

Philip's breath is felt on his back as the two of them make their way into the area where the clan leader will heal his daughter. He has the healing gift of Raphah given him by the Ancient of Days, millions of years ago, before the fall of his kind. He is the only remaining Nephilim with the gift.

Alexander personally slew seven of the ten Bachar, yet had been able to secure eight of the ten swords. Soon, he shall exam two others which he feels confident that at least one of them will be authentic. If both are, then his empire will certainly come forth with no opposition. The existing clans were instructed to move forward even if only one is found to be forged by the Ancient One. The time is at hand to challenge the Maseth; especially, with the promise of support from Prince Qadar. This fallen Seraph, with two others, will prove most valuable. Alexander will sit upon the throne of the new world empire, but Qadar will be the supernatural power behind all endeavors. Together they will succeed...they must succeed.

Both of the Nephilim move swiftly down the stairs and rush into the council room. In the eyes of man, this room is an oversized private bar and dining room. But to the Nephilim clan in Copper Town, it serves as a council room. In the supernatural realm, as now, it serves as a place for the Raphah to perform his healings.

Behind the Nephilim, the iridescent lighting of the garden fades, but not before the last of its flickering illumination reveals two other mystical beings following Alexander and Philip. Although they are supernatural with no created material substance, in pride and vanity they created a form in which they could walk among the Nephilim. Many years ago, they mined precious diamonds from the earth and molded them into vessels they could inhabit whenever it pleased them. Man's encounters with these Seraphs had left fables of robots and mechanical beings that could alter, or transform their shapes. But today, they take the form of men as they sweep past the Nephilim to stand as guardians beside the large double doors entering the council room. A massive golden beam has been placed into position to prevent entry.

On the west side of the room, a large fire burns; spitting forth flames of purple, green and orange. The flames rush outward beneath a large metallic altar which was positioned there prior to Alexander's arrival. The top of the slab is decorated with cold blue stones. This is the altar upon which the leader will perform Kara's healing. He wastes no time in removing the blood soaked blanket from his daughter. Her bare body is placed upon the altar and immediately the exposed blood sizzles before bursting forth throughout the room like bottle rockets on the fourth of July.

Kara's breathing stopped moments before, but the clan leader knows there is still time for healing, even from human standards. He steps back quickly and undresses. As his clothing drops to the floor, two other Nephilim sweep forward. They are large and clumsy in appearance; however, their movements are made with such graceful ease that they appear to be floating apparitions. They drape the crimson ceremonial robe upon their leader and step back to watch him perform that which he alone is capable of doing.

Alexander's hands move upon the blood soaked skin of his daughter who is part Nephilim and part human. She is the daughter of Alexander, the Nephilim leader of the Clan Shachar who has performed this rite since the founding of the world. First, he pushes her long blond hair back and blankets her face with his large hands. He would start with her mind. There he assures her of the healing that will take place and calls her drifting soul to return to the land of the living. Afterwards his hands move slowly, smoothly, and tenderly with small circling movements over her bloodiness. His hands move from one body part to another with healing. The restoration reveals her body afresh with no signs of blood, bruising or wounds. And underneath the skin all damaged tissue, bones and organs are renewed.

The occupants of the room are not surprised with what is taking place. They expected it to be so. Kara gasps, breathes deeply and sits up with her bright blue eyes shining like brilliant orbs amidst the dim lights of the room. She draws both legs beneath her and crosses them with no pretense of hiding her exposed body. Her arms rest across her knees. She sits in a trance-like state glaring at the room and those occupying it. She has been here before, but this is the first time she has been the recipient of her Father's gifting. Kara reaches up to meet the arms of Alexander as the two embrace. His created form may scare humans, but this is a form of her father she has seen often. Regardless of the shape he takes, her love for him will never be altered.

Tonight, his embrace reassures her of his undying love.

Chapter 16

A Snail's Pace

"The sluggard is wiser in his own conceit than
seven men that can render a reason."
Proverbs 26:16

Blue flickers of fire intertwined with green and purple fade slowly
before bursting forth with a transformation to bright orange, yellow
and red. The fire slowly ebbs but remains the only source of
luminosity. Its glistening and shimmering essence clambers from
the council room through the door and upward into the Nephilim
Garden. With a swift flick of his finger on the light switch,
Dormin floods the room with the harsh radiance of fluorescent
lights. The brightness flooding the room is a mere change in grays
for the Nephilim, but LeBazaja rubs her eyes squinting to allow her
pupils to adjust. As the room becomes more clearly visible to her,
she moves with quickness at the beaconing of her Nephilim mate
and wraps the exposed body of Kara with a blue cloak. A cloak
she has held in her hands throughout the ritual waiting for this
moment which she knew would come. At this point, human
participation is permissible. The brightness of light sends the
Seraph fleeing into their refuge of darkness. In their absence,

LeBazaja directs Kara to a small room near the rear of the Garden. Once inside, she will dress Alexander's daughter with the contents of the bag stored there.

Although LeBazaja enjoys tremendous human strength and her aging process has been thwarted through the mating with the Nephilim Dormin, she is familiar with the powers of Nephilim children known as Banah. Their powers were many times superior to hers. She envies this beautiful and perfect blond-haired image of a human. They had become close friends over the years and she had selected Kara's favorite clothing for this occasion: a loose under shirt that would allow her to move freely, a pair of her lace panties (it seemed as if that was the only kind she wore) and a pair of loose fitting jeans. The jeans were a little on the sloppy side for LeBazaja, yet they were unable to cloak the perfect feminine form beneath. She brought no bra for she knew Kara well enough to know she would simply toss it aside.

LeBazaja was well acquainted with the lustful eyes of men, and women, as they gazed upon the perfection of Kara. But, she was also aware of Alexander's threatening glare which kept the clan at bay for Nephilim also desired this Banah. His children were off limits for the whimsical needs of Nephilim pleasure. The Banah, including Alexander's children, often had intimate relationships with humans; but it was always for their pleasure or to accomplish some deed for which their fathers trained them.

LeBazaja accidentally brushes Alexander's arm as they start to exit the council room. She knows instantly her carelessness is a mistake.

Alexander swirls looming over her with intentions of tearing her body into threads. A deep growl issues from his throat. As he steps toward her, Dormin appears from nowhere and positions himself between them. A growl of his own rips through the room. It is not directed at Alexander, but at his mate. Nevertheless, it is an intercessory movement that saves her life. She is not permitted to touch any Nephilim without proper invitation…including her mate. Years of close proximity with the Nephilim has caused carelessness. This mistake she files in her mind while vowing to be more heedful. Her existence depends upon the adherence of the vow.

When alone tonight, she knew a stern lecture would spill from the lips of Dormin. LeBazaja realizes her mate has delivered her; however, she fully understands that if a decision has to be made between Alexander and she, Dormin would choose his leader. Such was the dedication of the members of Shachar. Alexander had no enemies within his clan now that Pavel had been beheaded by John Calvin in the Garden this morning.

The Council Chairman spins away and ascends the steps. Capable of moving with speeds that were only perceived as a blur to the human eyes, his pace is noticed by all in the council room as meticulous, careful and somewhat like those of a snail. None follow him, for they know where he is going. Alone in the soil of the Garden, he will meditate and rest from the vast depletion of his gifted virtue of Raphah.

Chapter 17

Bottled Water

"He that passeth by, and meddleth with strife belonging not to him, is like one that taketh a dog by the ears."
Proverbs 26:17

Rosie moves slowly through the Parsonage making her way directly to the balcony overlooking Main Street. Every single step is made possible only by an inner strength she did not realize she had. Her body feels as if it is not her own, nor does it react to the intents of her mind. Onward she plods until she reaches the rails of her balcony. Once there, she is unable to control the heaviness of her breathing; nonetheless, she anchors the weight of her body on the weathered railing to glare at Beth as she drives away. She watches until she turns left and disappears on the street of her and Philip's abode.

For a moment she imagines Beth paused long enough to look back at her in the rearview mirror before following the directions of her turn signal. And somewhere in the depths of her mind she feels as if she heard an eerie laugh escaping the confines of her car. The thoughts she desires to examine are erased from the monitor of her mind by the sound of Alexander's helicopter directly overhead. She twists her head sideways in an effort to view the aircraft above her porch roof. Soon it appears more distinctly to the south as it climbs the mountain slope to Alexander's home.

Collapsing backward into a chair, she remembers the tranquility and solitude she and her husband had enjoyed on this balcony. As she gives thanks for the moments spent here, the chair affirms her emotions by embracing her body with the comfort of its thick padding.

Since their arrival in Copper Town a few weeks ago, it was here she and Calvin spent early morning hours. He read and prepared his weekly sermons while she sat with a glass of tea and enjoyed watching him. Occasionally, she was invited to listen while he excitedly shared his thoughts with her.

Why did he leave me? She wonders.

No matter what Beth or anyone else in this God forsaken place says, she will never believe her husband abandoned her. She would get to the bottom of this, but she knows she must be alert and on her toes.

"From this day forth," she whispers. "I will prepare my own food and not eat or drink anything prepared by others - especially Beth."

She hears the helicopter at Alexander's home purring softly after landing. It reminds her of listening to her husband's Harley as he rode down the streets and into the parking lot. Within seconds, it soars downward toward her from the mountain top. Her heart leaps within her body for a second. Under the heavy medication she has sustained, she is unable to move to the wooden planks of the balcony's rail. She can only close her eyes and prepare for the crash she feels is coming. To her relief and peace of mind, the sound passes over the Casino roof where it seems to slow for a second before moving on to the helipad at the north side of the rear parking lot.

Safe now from what she thought would be a crash into the roof of her apartment, Rosie moves slowly into the living room and begins to rearrange things to assist in her newly formed plans. A large plant is moved to the side of the sofa where she normally sits to have coffee with Beth. A side table is moved to the other end and a trash can is relocated below it. Rosie wads several pieces of paper and places them in the can until it is half full. She would not be caught off guard or deceived again. As she often heard her mother say as I child, she too would "take the dog by the ears."

All opened containers of food are dumped into the garbage disposal along with raw vegetables and fruit. Rosie imagines they are probably already compromised. Somewhere deep within her soul, in an area she had never entered, Rosie finds new strength. Strength she feels growing steadily as the effects of the drugs slowly ebb from her body.

"I will solve this problem and get to the bottom of all this deceit," she swears.

Placing her hands on her hips, she stands with her back to the kitchen and the massive sealed door which leads into an area directly above the casino. The paint and wax constituting the door's seal bear witness that it has been years since this portal has been used. She whispers a prayer to a God she knows well and who she feels knew her before the foundation of the world. With an "amen" she does that which she has vowed not to do…she relaxes. It is a loud crash behind her that reminds her she has forgotten to be watchful. Startled and scared, she leaps forward away from the threatening sound; her heart pounds as she discovers she has been rendered helpless. Somewhere a thought emerges among the jumble of confusion racing through her mind: *perhaps this is one dog I should have left alone!*

Chapter 18

Revealed Deceits

"As a mad man who casteth firebrands, arrows, and death, So is the man that deceiveth his neighbour, and saith, Am not I in sport?"
Proverbs 26:18-19

Alexander climbs the long stairwell into the Garden. The span at the rear of the entry was erected in a semi-circle, resembling a rainbow which bridges the lower room to the upper. His breaths are deep, but not caused from a laborious pace; rather, from the complex thoughts weighing heavily on his mind. His body has never experienced exhaustion, but his soul was often tormented from his journey on this hopeless planet.

Onward he climbs. Each step rises nearly sixteen inches with a span of nearly twenty-four. More than double that of the humans, but human he is not. He is Nephilim.

The beautiful hand-fashioned marble surface of each step is etched deep with marks from the Nephilim's constant visits into the soils of Eden. His large feet find little room to spare while his massive shoulders slump in anger as he nears the top level. Long black talons at the end of his feet curve downward placing additional etchings to those already there. The sound of the scratching is spine-chilling and bears a similarity to that of a teacher abrasively raking long finger nails across a slate board. In a natural setting, the sound would serve as an alert to those hearing it; however, the Seraph dwelling within the Garden need no warning of his approaching their den. Fully aware of his entering, they also know the intent of his heart. Their approval is already stamped into the depths of his wondering mind.

Today, he will lay his cards on the table and deal with Rosie. Even if it means he may eventually take her life, or lose his own, he has decided he will reveal himself to her in his true form. He will have the woman of his desires for she is the one who will replace his mate who passed years ago. At the next Feast of the Nephilim, she will be his...even if he has to forcibly take her. He has weighed all consequences and is now willing to wager it all.

Within seconds, he approaches the large garden entry into the parsonage, stops and directs his palms towards the door. A small breeze drifts from his face and across his hands before seeping slowly through the door. The gentle puff of air noiselessly releases the door from its seal before it swings open in silence and settles softly upon rusty hinges. Alexander steps inside.

A door much larger than normal for humans still requires him to stoop while making his entry into the home of Rosie McGarney. Completely unaware of his presences, she stands with her back to him. Her eyes are glued to the western facing window as if she is in a trance. The Leader of Clan Shachar decides to awaken her with fear before revealing himself. He slams his foot to the floor with such force that the entire Gionni Casino shakes upon its foundation. Terrorized beyond description, she leaps away, which causes him much pleasure. There is no doubt in his mind that the Nephilim and the servants in the building know that the moment of truth has arrived. This is the moment in which he will reveal his true nature to the beautiful woman that bears his Sign of the Yada.

All the inhabitants of Copper Town have come to know Rosie by the name Alexander uses.

Rosie is the "Shining Blackness!"

Chapter 19

An Unexpected Surprise

"As a mad man who casteth firebrands, arrows, and death, So is the man that deceiveth his neighbour, and saith, Am not I in sport?"
Proverbs 26:18-19

Alexander revels with pleasure watching Rosie leap toward the window. Her right fist, in an effort to thwart her momentum, smashes through the window pane. Small slashes in her flesh begin quickly to fill with blood. Withdrawing her slender bloody arm, she spins to face the beast standing before her. Her fear fades to anger and disgust. She assumes an aggressive stance suggesting she is prepared to defend herself. With legs flexed, she is ready to spring forward at the hideous giant standing in her kitchen. Her thoughts turn to the story of David and Goliath and like the little shepherd boy she shows no fear in the face of her Philistine foe. If there is any surprise, it is in the eyes of the Nephilim who watches as she defiantly opens her mouth to be the first to speak.

"So, Alexander…this is how you want me to know you?"

Centuries of walking along side of man has not prepared this ancient being for her response.

How could she know? He thinks. *How could she know?*

Spontaneously, and perhaps without intent, Alexander changes to the human form he has used since the Ancient of Days created man and then as quickly he returns to his true form. It is a display of power meant to startle her and cause her fear to return. To his surprise, it does not.

"I have encountered your kind before and I am not without understanding of your existence. The Book of the Maseth has explained your kind in many ways although most men do not discern it. I recognize it and I know who you are!"

Alexander pauses, his eyes locked with hers before answering.

"Let it be so, my little one. Then let it be so! Come, let us sit down and reason with that knowledge. We will gain understanding so that we shall move forth this day with wisdom and…with life!"

Rosie answers taking no thought of her words, "For the last week or so, I have dreamed dreams given me by the Old One. And like others before me, I have come to some understanding. The run through the park, the attack of the bikers, and my healing in the council room…all of these have I remembered. Your appearance is not new to me, I have seen you before in my dreams and I know my dreams are revelations to my soul. I know you. My body bears both your scar and that of your repugnant friend, Slim.

There is no difference between you and him, other than he does not mask his evil nature. It would be better for you if you were not lukewarm!"

Alexander recognizes the words and her meaning for speaking them. More realistically, he understands the spiritual intent of words written hundreds of years ago by the Ancient One. Now, they are directed at him.

Making no reply, he decides to stare her down. In so doing, he displays walrus-size incisors. Teeth that could, and had, ripped the head from many a man. They are more threatening than she remembered.

Rosie makes one cautious and daring step toward the Nephilim. Alexander counters with lightning speed and to her amazement his body is within inches of hers. For the first time, she displays genuine fear. Tilting her head upward to look into the dark fiery eyes glaring down at her, she is able to frame words that emerge from her throat.

"Where is John Calvin? What have you done with him? I know he did not leave me alone here, he would never do that."

Alexander is quick and defiant with his answer.

"At this very moment he is on his little motorcycle headed back to Riley. He thinks no one knows where he is and is unaware that the very strangers he entertains along the way are those I have sent to see that he arrives unscathed. Yet, when I get what I need, his body will return to the dust from which it came. My little Rosie, soon he will no longer hold a claim to you. Until that happens, I promise you I will honor the vows of your union. Afterwards, you will be mine regardless of how you feel. Affection is not important and in time you will come to appreciate all that I can do for you that no human man can do."

Suppressing both the tears in her eyes and the lump in her throat, Rosie grits pearly white teeth which shin brightly in the pool of her beautiful ebony face. Then, she spits upward into the face of the Nephilim. Alexander makes no effort to avoid the spittle spattering on his forehead. With long fingers supporting large talons, his hand moves leisurely upward as if he is going to wipe it away. Instead, he deliberately smears the spittle downward across his face leaving a fresh coat of dampness from her fluids. He breathes deep and tilts his head backward addressing the tall ceilings with a laugh. If he were to stand completely erect, his body would pierce the roof above. Eyes that had witnessed much of creation, and its fall from grace, look down upon her as a mother would look down at her newborn child. He smiles again and licks her spittle from his hand. One at a time, his fingers enter his mouth as he cleanses each from the juices of her body.

"Ummmm!" he cries with delight. "This is only a teasing sample of what I will have when you are mine!"

The act insights Rosie's anger and she is quick to let him know, "I'd rather die than to live my life with you! If John Calvin dies, I'll live to see your head severed from your monstrous body."

Alexander assumes his human form; however, his smile does not change. He turns toward the open portal to exit, but before doing so he looks back over his shoulder and leaves her with his rebuttal.

"That may be an option for you...maybe...maybe not! Time will tell, but within a couple of weeks, little Rosie, your dearly beloved will depart from this life. Until then, you will not leave this dwelling. That is not a request and you will do as you are told. If not, be prepared to pay the consequences!"

Chapter 20

Hints of Fiery Red Splashes

" Where no wood is, there the fire goeth out: so where there is no talebearer, the strife ceaseth."
Proverbs 26:20

"Hello Handsome…room for two in that little tent?"

Len teases knowing her words will not return void. She drove like a mad woman to get here expecting to hear any moment that he had left and she would have to turn around to catch up with him westward on I-40. Like a war eagle, she gazes down at the man sitting on the ground outside his tent.

With heavily muscled arms, he reaches inside the tent and drags out an old, but clean, pair of jeans. Stuffing both feet into the waist, he sluggishly pushes them through the legs until they are exposed again. Afterwards, he dawdles at standing and pulling them to his waist. The leisure he takes in dressing is to permit her a view of his jockey underwear. Her blue eyes climb his legs along with the jeans as they slide upward. Her inspection stops briefly at the junction of his lower limbs; then continues upward to her true objective, his eyes. She cannot maintain the gaze and elects to drop her eyes, once again, to examine his underwear.

Dave notices the object of her stare. He slowly zips his fly and fastens his belt. Bending down to retrieve a brilliant white shirt, he slips it on and fastens only the bottom three buttons. His decision not to tuck it is formulated by his thoughts. *It won't be long before I'm getting out of this...no need in getting too comfortable.*

Having dressed, he answers her question. "There's always room for a beautiful lady like you. What's on your mind?"

He had laid lazily in the tent after being awakened around four p.m. to the sound of a motor home parking adjacent to his tent site. Through the mesh screen window of his tent, he observed this woman moving with astonishing speed to make the connections to her motor home. She rarely took her eyes from his camp site. His assumption was incorrect in thinking that the chrome splendor of his bike had caught her eye. She had a beautiful feminine body with long thick hair that bounced in the sunlight like fiery red flames. He longed to grasp her mane in his hands and had vowed an hour ago, "Before the night is over, she will lie in my arms."

"Well," she says, "I thought we might take a spin into town for dinner and perhaps afterwards we could watch a movie at my place. That is, if you think you are up to it?"

"I'm up to it. Just give me time to take a shower and we'll ride out."

Len smiles and invites him with, "Come on over and use my shower. It will be cleaner and more…private."

Dave looks at the duffle bag he tossed into his tent earlier. Not for protection, but to conceal the swords he was toting.

He answers the red haired girl, "Give me a second to grab a few items. By the way, my name is Dave."

What's with names? Len muses. *And who really cares*? *Wouldn't he be surprised that I already know who he is?*

She laughs turning to make her way back to her motor home.

"Okay Dave, I'm Len. Come on over when you're ready."

Walking towards her Intrigue she turns once again to inspect the body of this man she has been dispatched to kill. Every inch and characteristic of his body is etched within her mind. She closes her eyes and views them again with her photographic memory.

Well, well…She muses from the review, *I will not be in a rush tonight. I'm going to have a little pleasure before completing my assignment!*

She envisions a cat playing with a mouse for hours before the kill and promises herself that before the night is over, she will do the same!

Chapter 21

The Straight Gate

"As coals are to burning coals, and wood to fire;
so is a contentious man to kindle strife."
Proverbs 26:21

A westward wind crawls softly down the long narrow gorge of the canyon. It carries a stench she easily recognizes. Yet, she dares not tilt her head and open her nostrils from fear that the one hiding on the ledge will observe her detection. She knows the unpleasant smell is that of a human and catches sight of him peeking over a large bolder watching her every move. Little does he know that it is she who has planned their destiny.

She places one hoof before the other to make her way upward through the canyon to the top of the rim rock. From there, she often observed the desert floor below. On many occasions she had detected assailants and escaped over the mountain long before they approached her sacred bedding grounds. Dominant winds combining with thermal drifts have been ignored by the one hiding above. His ignorance will serve her needs.

Foolishly, the man on the ledge smirks with joy thinking he has outsmarted her tonight. His fantasies will soon be shattered like china falling from a cupboard.

A cool wisp of wind sends shivers along her back and over her flanks. Not shivers of dread, but of delight in anticipation of her well conceived plan. The blood, of her ancestors, flows untainted through her veins. She is of Spanish decent and for centuries her kind has roamed this area of the southwest; never breeding with the wild clans which escaped from early settlers. Roan bristles sparkle from her perspiration giving highlight to the white strands interwoven with her beautiful brown coat. She pauses for a second to enjoy the sounds of nature and to allow the fragrance of the fresh desert blossoms to erase the disgusting odor.

When the moment comes, she will allow this human to think he caught her by surprise, but the surprise will be hers. She quivers again from the foreplay of a scene that will soon unfold. Cautiously, she moves. She must not let him know she is aware of his presence. Her heart beats faster and thumps within her breast like a drum pounding in the night. The musk of his body causes her lungs to swell. As her breathing becomes shallow, it causes her body to tremble from the decreasing flow of blood. Her body temperature soars with anticipation and her emotions glow like hot coals encouraged by a soft breeze flowing through puckered lips. Like two humans facing each other with swords in mortal combat, she too is ready. To the victor go the spoils…so let the ride begin!

Chapter 22

Eating Ashes beneath the Roast

"The words of a talebearer are as wounds, and they go down into the innermost parts of the belly."
Proverbs 26:22

"This will not be my first," he whispers as a soft chuckle attempts to erase the apprehension swelling in the core of his body.

The element of surprise will be his when she arrives from below into the narrow passage beneath him; a passage barely wide enough for her to pass.

She, on the other hand, is slowly working upward to her bedding grounds along the upper ledges of the canyon walls. Since birth, she was taught to use the cliffs for observation of the valley while utilizing predominant winds from the rear to detect any approaching threats from above. Tonight, they warn her of the ambush.

Apprehensively, she continues the pace upward. Looking down into the sandy floor of her mountain pass, she notices the canyon floor exhibits wear from many years of use. Now, another set of prints are added to establish her ownership.

The man waiting on her appreciates the desires of all before him who have attempted to ride this beautiful, magnificent beast. Many endeavored to tame and possess her but all failed.

"Tonight," he vows, "she will be mine!"

He assures himself that she is unaware of his presence. Within moments she will be directly below him. Blood courses through his body and he trembles uncontrollably from the rush of adrenalin. The palms of his hands become moist with sweat.

"It is time," he declares softly!

With a swift leap, he commits himself to the flight before him. Downward he continues with legs spread wide with her back as his target. But upon the point of expected contact, he is shocked watching her move ahead rapidly as if she knew his intent. As a result, he lands on her flanks.

In haste, he falls forward across her back and with his left arm reaches beneath her and clings to her stomach. With the fingers of his right hand, he clutches the thick blood red hair of her mane and prepares for the ride of his life. The force of her upward buck makes him feel as if he is the one that has been mounted. Throbbing pain burst from his groin. His pain pulsates into pleasure as it becomes secondary to his excitement. He embraces her tighter with his arms and legs; slowly, he slides his inner thighs upward along her back.

She leaps upward against the force of his demands. His heaviness is exciting and she turns teasingly to nibble his leg. In the depths of her mind, she realizes care must be given not to dislodge this rider too soon. She must not cause him to be fearful or he might abandon the wildness of the ride and bail off. It is enough to let him know that she can, and very well might, inflict more pain sometime during this wild ride. She leaps forward and with several rapid successive thrusts, she begins to drain him of his energy. Her wild reactions are ceaseless and offer no hint of relaxation to the rider pressing against her back. With both legs she kicks upward into the night before sliding sideways to bruise his leg against the rocky wall of the canyon. To her surprise, he still maintains a somewhat precarious seat astride her and his embrace indicates he will not be quickly deposed. She is pleased for this is the physical match she has long awaited.

She continues grinding against the weight of her rider and laboriously inches her way into an open area of the canyon. There she finds room to perform the executions that have been successful for her in the past. She drops to her knees only to discover that her rider is vigorously kicking at her flanks with his heels. With a jarring thud, she drops to her stomach and begins to roll. She and her rider exchange positions continuously until the soft sandy bed merges with the hard surface of the canyon wall. With all these efforts, she has still failed to dislodge him.

He maintains the deep grip of her flowing mane and his arm embraces her tighter than before. Once again, he wonders if it is she who will tame him. Many years of his childhood were spent in preparing him to become a man; those years would not be wasted now. He will hang on and show this beast that he is the one who is in command. He slides up her back again; this time with more ease due to the mingling of their sweat. He bites the tip of her ear for she is not the only one with teeth and she will not be the only one permitted their use. Unlike her teasing nip, he sinks his teeth deep within her skin and watches as blood oozes from the wound. It flows forth in a large bubble before it spills like a crimson river down her neck.

The smell of blood, especially her own, intensifies and arouses her to greater heights of excitement. She bucks harder gasping for the breath which has escaped her swollen lungs. Her loud moans, ushering forth from the innermost parts of her stomach, join with the exclamation of his delight. Together, they perform a sensual duet of perfect harmony.

Again she acclimates and reassesses the situation. "No, this will not be as easy as I thought, but the pleasure of the ride has already exceeded any experiences I have encountered in the past!"

Onward the two battle for dominance of position throughout the night. One series of moves after another is performed without thought. When all familiar moves are spent, they duplicate those previously performed. The floor of their arena is crumpled and wrinkled like paper; yet its rugged and torn appearance gives no hint of which will emerge victorious. Somewhere in the long night, she surrenders from exhaustion.

Falling for the last time to a position of defeat, she releases the pressure swollen within her. Like a volcano, she explodes; completely exhausted and helpless beneath him. Her life is now in his hands, but she is beyond caring. Sleep is what she seeks…and beneath him, she falls into a sleep she has never experienced.

Chapter 23

Reflections

"Burning lips and a wicked heart are like a
potsherd covered with silver dross."
Proverbs 26:23

Rolling over softly, but not without effort, Dave glances at the
clock on the dresser. The large digital display reads 04:55 AM.
He lies still for a moment to force remembrance of a fading dream.
It was a dream of a young Indian boy who became a brave by
riding a wild mustang mare that no other brave had ridden. His
mother told the story to him when he was a mere child. He often
envisioned himself as that young boy; especially, in the company
of wild women. Tonight, in the bed of this auburn haired wonder,
he had lived the dream.

Glancing over his shoulder, he sees the nude body of Len
lying atop her satin sheets, her back to him. Brilliant red hair
flows over her shoulders and down her back like an invitation for
him to awaken her.

He had gotten only a couple hours of sleep, but it had been
the most enjoyable night of his life. In his mind, he reviews the

plans he made earlier that day. She was not a part of those plans, so he decides it is time to take his leave from her. Somewhere in the night, they had discussed the feasibility of traveling together since they were both headed west. But, Dave had no time for companionship, especially that of a female. Besides, a motor home was not his favorite means of travel. If he hurried, he could make Durango, Colorado with enough day light remaining to tour a cliff dwelling he wanted to see before continuing on to Copper Town.

For a moment, memories from the previous evening invade his mind. After showering last evening in Len's motor home, he stepped from behind the glass door into her bedroom with intentions of dressing before dinner. Dave had longed for a good meal since he had not eaten in a couple of days. Time coupled with a tight growl in his stomach, had informed him that he was now three days into unplanned fasting. Yet, when he stepped from the shower, the clothes he had placed on the bed were gone. In their place was the red haired woman…lying leisurely and naked upon her bed. He had never spent a night with such furious and wild sensual pleasures. Now, he confesses, he is tired and has muscles aching in places he never knew existed.

Grudgingly, he stares at Len's naked and exhausted body as she lies sleeping contentedly. He confesses that, perhaps, it was she who had emerged victorious last night.

A forbidden fantasy races through his mind but is dismissed quickly. He cannot indulge himself any more, for there is no time to clean up afterward. So, he decides to let her continue in her slumbers.

Quietly he eases to a sitting position on the edge of the bed.

I'll just dress, sneak out, pack my gear and head west...alone, he thinks.

Silently he makes a vow. *The burning lips of this woman will never scorch my soul again. I am finished with her!*

Yet, he pauses before admitting. *For a woman, she has strength and power like no other...not even Lisa. If I didn't have more pressing things to do, I might just spend a little more time with her before...*

Chapter 24

A Mirror's Betrayal

"He that hateth dissembleth with his lips, and
layeth up deceit within him;"
Proverbs 26:24

Ever so softly, though he feels an earthquake could not awaken Len, Dave sits up on the side of the bed looking at his reflection in the mirror. Over his shoulder he is able to view the large brilliant orb of a near full moon. He wonders why he did not notice it last night. Then he smiles with full acknowledgement that he had noticed nothing outside the realm of lustful passion. Time is slipping by and he can linger no longer in the bed of this red haired wonder.

He slips from the mattress and within seconds is dressed. He returns to the edge of the bed and quietly sits, once more, to put on his boots. Bending over, he retrieves the first boot and places it in his lap. He decides to carry them to the tent site before putting them on simply because his ritual of lacing is tedious and aggressive. To do it here would surely awaken her. Before retrieving the other boot, he straightens up on the bed for one last view of the moon that had perched in the mirror like a parrot on his shoulder. Dave had seen a lot of terrible and horrific things in his life, but none had prepared him for the reflection in the mirror. His heart skips a beat and chill bumps cover his body; he shudders violently with fearful hesitation. The hesitation is only for a fraction of a moment, but it comes close to being his last.

Instead of the bright globe of the moon, Dave sees Len within inches of the back of his head. Her eyes are glowing as bright as the crimson of her hair and bright sparkles of yellow coals dance within them. Her mouth opens wider than Dave imagines possible as she displays teeth that are not human. Her upper canines are twice as long as the others protruding slightly outward from her mouth. Like a viper, her head moves forward to sink those fangs deep into the side of his neck. With lightning speed, Dave shoves the boot upward to intercept the strike; with no time to spare. Her teeth sink deep into the thick man-made material of the sole where they become embedded. Unlike him, she does not hesitate. She reaches downward over his shoulders with both arms and sinks long talon-like finger nails into his chest. Fingers that earlier left trails of passion on his back, now seek to rip his heart from his chest.

She, too, had enjoyed the night, but the time of passion has passed. The cat has toyed with the mouse long enough. Now, the time has come to rid herself of this human she was sent to destroy.

Dave uses the mirror to assist him in his defense. He grabs the hellcat's wrists with his hands. Yanking them from his flesh, he watches blood flow in the mirror. Her face is distorted and no longer displays the beauty he knew. She shakes the boot rapidly from side to side like a dog in an attempt to free it from her mouth. It is the only option she has with her hands gripped in his. Her actions are not without reward. The boot crashes into the wall with a loud thud. Scratches are left on the polished wood paneling, but not before Len recoils for another strike with her fangs. This time as she snaps downward, Dave sends her naked body over his head by swinging her arms upward and away from his. His counter move is more to prevent her teeth from penetrating his neck than a premeditated defensive move; however, it adequately serves as both.

Her collision with mirror shatters it into hundreds of sharp shards which fall to the dresser top before spilling onto the carpet. Several are embedded in the perfection of her flesh which immediately spews forth blood. Her body, as it thumps to the top of the dresser, seems more like a surreal piece of art than that of a woman. Len does not fall into a crumpled heap to Dave's surprise. She instantly rolls from the dresser and leaps toward him. This time her teeth sink deep into an exposed target; the meaty muscle of his right inner thigh, inches from his groin. Although that had not been the object of her strike, she is satisfied with the proximity and locks her jaws tight. A hold she vows to maintain until she can exchange it for his throat. She feels flesh tearing from his leg caused by the forcefulness of her bite.

With his left hand, Dave seizes her long hair in a futile attempt to remove her fangs. At the same time, Len reaches up and grabs his hair. She tugs hard to bring his head close to hers. If she can manage that task, she will quickly exchange his leg for his neck. Once that is accomplished, she will rip the jugular vein from his throat. Then she will allow his blood to spill into her mouth and across her body as she watches him die. A fiendish laugh gurgles through clenched teeth while her body grows with increasing strength inflamed by her thoughts of taking his life. It is a feat Len has executed more than once.

Unbeknownst to her, Dave is no stranger to taking life either. His days on earth have been less than hers, but the number of lives he has taken, far surpasses hers. As she pulls his head slowly downward, he smashes the side of her face with his right fist. The force of his punch frees his leg from her locked bite. Her body flies to the side but is prevented from crashing into the wall by the tight grip on his hair which she maintains. Her attempt to smile at him is useless. The river of blood flowing from her mouth and nose cannot cloak the missing canine that was left embedded deep within his thigh.

Len was unaware that pain of this magnitude existed. She looks into the eyes of Dave and realizes what will soon come to pass. Furthermore, she knows she is no match against this human and is puzzled as from what source this mere mortal draws such power.

It will be her last thoughts, for a vicious onslaught of Dave's right hand delivers blow after blow into the depths of what was once a beautiful face. The transformation that takes place from the assault leaves her head as nothing but a bloody and unrecognizable lump.

The uncontrollable and vicious attack is slow to ease. Knowing she is dead, he continues to punch her face as a boxer pounds a punching bag. Even when he ceases, the soldier desires to continue the beating. As he looks upon the corpse of the woman he held passionately a few hours ago, he feels no remorse. She is only a woman: weak and deserving that which she received. During the course of the night, he thought she might be one that was different. But now look at her!

"You're just like all the others," he says aloud. Her crumpled body reminds him briefly of Lillie.

He met Miss Lillie in Paris while on a month deployment working in the U.S. Embassy. He was attracted to her at a small street café when he noticed how lively she stepped and heard the joy in her laughter. She had sat at a small table with two other women speaking in French, which he did not understand. His work was highly classified and he had not been sent there to socialize with the locals. After the departure of Lillie's two female companions, she waved at him and uttered a greeting.

By necessity, he laughed, shrugged his shoulders and said, "I do not speak French!"

Miss Lillie, as he soon began to call her, was an unmarried elementary school teacher who enjoyed the night life of her city. She laughed again and extended a greeting in English. Her broken English often required assistance from him; but within days, they discovered several things they enjoyed beyond the scope of what nightfall provided. One was base jumping; a thrill of free falling before pulling the cord to your chute at the last minute possible. Dave was been pleasantly surprised to find a woman who enjoyed it. He felt that base jumping was mainly for men; although a few women participated in the sport, they were still the minority.

Dave and Lillie had both soared from the cliffs of Kjerag, on Lysefjord in Norway and constantly joked about taking the trip to Pakistan's Trango Towers. Although they teased about doing it, Dave never told her he had actually done it. Both had jumped from bridges too numerous to list.

Lillie confessed that one day she planned to tour the U.S. and if the opportunity presented itself, she would love to jump from two sites. One was man-made and the other was natural, but both were illegal. She dreamed of both, the El Capitan in Yosemite National Park and the St. Louis Arch. Dave dared not tell her, but he had also jumped from both of those in the darkness of night and while alone. Thus, he had no one to report him. Jumping, to Dave was not about the publicity, but the personal thrill of the fall.

He presented Miss Lillie with the challenge one night in asking, "If you would dare to go to the U.S. and make those illegal jumps, why have you not jumped from the Eiffel?"

She grinned and threw up her hand toward the tower. "It is very heavily guarded. Much more so, I think, than in America. Besides, I suppose things in your own country are not as challenging or thrilling as those in another land."

"Let's do it!" Dave dared.

Lillie was like him, she wanted no publicity, fame or fortune. She, too, lived for the thrill of victory. To get caught would certainly be her agony of defeat and the heavy fine would exceed her income. Beyond that, she would lose her job. But under his constant urging, she consented. After planning it carefully, the two made their way to the upper level of the tower. They had posed as artists with packs of canvases, oil paints, and easels which concealed their small chutes.

After the fall of darkness, they slipped upward over the protective fence barrier and climbed to the girders above. For the first time in their brief relationship, Dave detected fear in Lillie. Her knuckles were white as she clung tightly to the heavy riveted metal beam trying to slip her chute on. Both knew at this height, of around 1000 feet, they would have only three seconds of free-fall before pulling the cords of their parachutes. Both knew also, they had to make a strong leap outward to clear the base of the third level which curved slightly outward. They had chosen the side that would allow a moderate breeze to help them drift away from the tower. Their landing and proposed route of escape was also planned.

Placing the chute over her shoulders, she was ready to snap the first of two latches when Dave reached over, grabbed her arm and slung her outward away from the tower. It was more than enough to assist her in clearing the lower levels. He laughed as she sailed away from him in the dark. But looking down, he knew he made an error in the launching of Miss Lillie. Her body spun over as she plummeted backward, which allowed him to see the shock displayed on her face. It was a shock from which she never recovered.

To demonstrate what she should have done, he leapt from the beam with both of his chute latches unfastened. He turned backward as she had, quickly fastened both latches and immediately pulled the cord. The opened chute permitted him to observe Lillie's final descent. She bumped the base of the third level and crashed downward toward the larger base of the second one. There, she disappeared like a steel ball in a pinball machine, bumping and careening through the girders until her body landed with a horrific and bloody plop on the sidewalk.

Although Dave had abandoned Lillie that night, he was arrested the next day because the jump had been recorded by security cameras installed on the tower. That had been the end of his military career for he was forced into early retirement. He was not troubled by the Army's decision since he received full retirement benefits.

When it came to Miss Lilly's death, he was satisfied with his own explanations, "She had been weak; much weaker than he desired. People like her should never dare to do things like base jumping. Such weakness can never be rewarded by pleasure or long life. She deserved the death she experienced."

It was not the way his parents had taught him. They preached compassion and meekness. He, on the other hand, believed in power and ascribed his philosophical beliefs to those of the Stoics.

"Emotions," he believed, "can never be employed in determining the path one must follow to enjoy the peace from all the trials that life throws at you. You must survive."

He had been forced from one missionary field to another by his parents. He learned early to play the game, to talk the talk, but the walk was never his. Through lies and deceits he masked the truth that was dormant within until he was old enough to escape the grappling hooks of his parents. At age seventeen, he had persuaded them to sign permission forms for him to join the Army. It was there that he found himself and became the man he was destined to be.

The thoughts of Lillie fade when Dave stares at Len's bloody body. He celebrates with a shout of victory to the dead corpse, "See...I am not my father's son!"

Chapter 25

Faithfulness Tested

"When he speaketh fair, believe him not: for there
are seven abominations in his heart."
Proverbs 26:25

Like a caged tiger, Rosie paces the floor. For over two weeks she
has been imprisoned in a home she thought would be her and
Calvin's sanctuary until they retired to their hometown of Riley,
Tennessee. Her steps have been like stars in the sky, too numerous
to count. Additionally, they have worn deep paths into carpeted
areas and rubbed finish from the ones with hardwood flooring.
Sleep has, for the most part, evaded her. The lack of it has not
been from fear for she is anxious to strike the beast who claimed to
have slain her husband. Yesterday, he sent her the note which she
holds crumpled in her fist.

Near the window she broke a couple of weeks ago; she
stops to read it again. The setting sun shines brightly through the
western side of her living room and she knows the bright rays will
soon disappear into the flat lands of the desert. As of now, it
serves as the only source of illumination for her eyes.

After she smashed the window, Alexander replaced it the very next day with a larger and more elaborate one. It measured nearly six feet wide by six feet high with a clear square center of four feet. A one foot perimeter of stained glass, featuring Christian themes, bordered the center section. It was an overt attempt to appease her. If Rosie had known what was involved with the construction of the window, she might have been more appreciative.

It had taken an entire family business, along with all their employees, working around the clock in Reno to complete it by the deadline given them by the Nephilim leader. They had labored hard for the large cash bonus of having it finished by daylight. But the timely completion was due more from the fear for their lives if they failed to complete the project. Jim flew up the night before in the helicopter to be available to transport it back as soon as it was completed.

Nor did Rosie know that she had endangered the lives of the repairmen on the following morning by refusing to let them work from inside the parsonage. Her ban forced them to use long ladders and scaffolding to remove broken glass and splintered wood along with the old window frame. She observed wrinkles of worry stamped upon their brows. If the glass had been broken, none of them would have lived to see the sun go down. The little Latino, Antonio, was one of the men employed to complete the renovation of the wall. Antonio was the sole operator of the crematory located across the street. When not busy inside the building, Antonio maintained a beautiful garden in the adjacent lot. Both operations were owned by Alexander.

Antonio laughed occasionally while watching Rosie open sealed containers of food. She refused to eat anything in her pantry, or delivered to her door; especially by Beth. She drank only bottled water which had been stored earlier in her pantry. On occasions, Rosie tried to communicate with Antonio. Even when she thought he understood, he laughed and affirmed the fact that he did not.

"Me, no speak English," was always his one and only reply.

Maybe, just maybe, she had dared to hope, *he is one I can trust!*

She unfolds the note and reads it aloud once again.

My dear sweet Rosie,

Soon, you will be mine regardless of your desire. I have set you free from your husband and the ashes of his body have returned to the dust from whence they came. Weigh carefully your response to what I now present you with. I must have your answer by noon today. Although you have lost a husband, there remains another whom you love: your only son David. If you do not surrender with a voluntary yes to become my mate, then by nightfall he too will join his father. His life is in your hands. My mark, which you bear in your flesh, cannot be removed; nor, will I release my claim upon you. I will not free you from our union. Choose quickly...and choose wisely. –

Alexander

She had given Beth, who delivered the note and waited upon her reply, her answer.

"Tell that monster," she screamed, "I said NEVER!"

As much as she loved her son, she could never give in to the desires of such wickedness.

Rosie watched her son grow up with the loving eyes of a mother. She noticed at an early age, he was not interested in religion, nor did he seriously indulge in their ceremonial practices. Often, she had made intercession for her son to protect him from the stern lectures which John Calvin gave liberally. When he was a teenager, she placed him in the care of a God he did not know. She often cried out in prayer for her son's deliverance and safety. Her reply yesterday to Beth was no exception. If what the clan leader told her was true, David was better off in the hands of God than in Alexander's. Regardless of how Alexander might speak to her, with threats or with flowery words of kindness and promises, she knew him to be an evil creature. One that could not be trusted for his heart was dark and abominable. Nonetheless, she had promised to remain faithful to a God she knew to be Sovereign in all things.

When Alexander heard the report from Beth, he laughed and spoke softly. But, his words were heard by all in the council room.

"My little Rosie has passed the first test much better than her husband!"

He turns to look at his daughter. Continuing with his laughter, he slaps her on the back and asks, "Is that not right Kara?"

His daughter laughs also and without speaking a word she nods her head with affirmation.

Chapter 26

A Nephilim Sermon

"Whose hatred is covered by deceit, his
wickedness shall be shewed before the whole
congregation."
Proverbs 26:26

Reminding her of a sitcom, three loud raps echoes down the
hallway of the parsonage and Rosie hears the voice of the
Nephilim bellowing from outside with a loud, "ROSIE!"

Her spine stiffens with aggravation and disgust from the
sound of the Council Chairman. Nevertheless, she moves quickly
to open the door expecting to face the giant Nephilim form of
Alexander. The sun is shining bright in the early evening hours
and, perhaps, she has forgotten that these vampire-like creatures
can only walk in the day by taking on the form of a human. No
doubt if nightfall had enveloped the little town, she would have
witnessed the original created form of the Nephilim leader.

Wrenching the door open, it bangs against the freshly
painted wall sending several fragments of plaster falling like snow
to the entry floor. Her eyes are aflame with hatred for this creature

who claims he has taken the life of her husband. Yet as she glares into his dark orbs, she discovers he does not share her feelings. Deep within his eyes, she sees a growing love for her that goes beyond human explanations. The very thought of this creature touching her repels her so much, that she struggles to remain logical. This only adds to the rage that burns deep within her heart. She does not reply but her emotions are clearly revealed when she stares into his eyes.

"Rosie, may I come in? It is time for us to talk."

"If I say no, will you not simply barge in anyway?"

"Yes I will," he replies. "But I would rather this visit be more cordial and amenable. It is time for us to stop avoiding the unspoken issues between us."

The widow of John Calvin McGarney steps aside to allow entry into her abode taking care that the Nephilim does not touch her ebony skin. Skin on which he has left a tiny scar that claims he has a right to take her as his mate. Close to the tiny circular scar is a second one that was left by Slim. Slim was no longer a rival since John Calvin severed his head from his body. Alexander and Slim would have fought to the death in order that the victor could claim Rosie as his mate.

Alexander moves quietly, as if he is floating, and with swiftness to the kitchen table. His movements are not generated by speed, but simply by his willed ability to move a few seconds ahead of Rosie in time. The human female that follows him only imagines some miracle has taken place. Needlessly done to impress her for it does not. Rosie has no fear of this creature.

She sits at the opposite end of the little dining room table and glares at Alexander. For days she has been in prayer and now she knows her petitions have been answered.

Come boldly before the throne of grace, she remembered…and had done so. Her boldness had pleased her redeemer and he had privately revealed more to her than the Nephilim could imagine.

There is a small stirring of her mind and her soul rises to barricade the invasion it knows is coming from the creature opposite her as he attempts, once again, to read her thoughts. And once again, he fails, accepting the fact that this one is truly a chosen vessel of the Ancient of Days. She is a member of the Maseth by no choosing of her own, thus her mind is protected from him as long as she remains faithful to her God's purpose. Alexander has vowed he will entangle her into his world, thus removing the protective shield that stands between them. Or, he will risk his very life to force her against her will to mate with him.

"What is it you want, Son of Perdition?"

Alexander laughs and as the hideous sound thunders into the room, he slams both fists atop the table. Seams of wood that were glued by some unknown carpenter are weakened by the force of his fists; yet, they hold as if they have declared an alliance with the woman.

"I think you have your theology somewhat mixed up my sweet little lady, but soon you will meet the true son of Qadar. He is alive and ready to ascend to the throne of the empire we have collectively planned since the creation of your kind. Do not be deceived, he is not a weak offspring of mine and your kind, but has a higher creation as his father. Yes, my dear, very soon you along with the world will come to know the power of a human who is the son of a true Cherub."

An expressionless woman sits quietly before him. He cannot read her thoughts, neither does he know, all this has been revealed to Rosie.

"Rosie, Nephilim are not fallen angels as some of you ignorant religious people believe. We were created millions of years before man. You may find that surprising, or unbelievable, but just think what your Tablet of the Maseth teaches…that one day with the Ancient One is as a thousand years, and a thousand years is as one day."

Alexander gloats with pride that he has quoted from her Tablet. Actually, he had it memorized…word for word. He knew more about her Tablet and the God she served than she would ever know in her life time.

"Are you familiar with that?" he asks.

"It's from an epistle written by Saint Peter," she snaps back. A great deal of humility is detected from her response and it is intended only as acknowledgement of what she knows to be truth.

The Nephilim continues, "Okay, listen to me, if the average human life span today is sixty-seven years then roughly that equates to twenty-four thousand, four hundred seventy-two days. If each one of those is as a thousand years in the eyes of the Ancient One, you are looking at twenty-four million, four hundred seventy-two thousand years in eternity. Not much time at all really. If you take the age of the Earth since the original creation, which your Genesis rightly contributes to God, you will find it nearly four and a half billion years old. Since the beginning, other creations walked this world until Qadar lead a rebellion and destroyed most of the life forms. They were not human. Man was created around six thousand years ago with the restoration, or as your book says *the replenishing of the Earth.* Man was created in the likeness of the Ancient of Days."

"I tell you this so that you might believe when I say that I have walked this planet for nearly twenty million years. If you divide that by a thousand, you'll get twenty thousand days. If I may, I have divided those days by three hundred sixty-five and three fourths to come up with a human equivalence of about fifty-five. Time is only relevant to you humans who do not understand eternity; even though it has been taught to you."

The woman opposite him shakes her head and finally contributes to the conversation.

"You are playing word games with numbers. I may understand the teachings of time in its perspective of God more than you realized! If Adam had not rebelled against God in the

112

Garden of Eden, he would still be alive and would have never died!"

Alexander gives a nod of consent, convinced she still does not understand.

"My beautiful Shining Blackness, I don't think you grasp anything about us or who we are. We have walked among you and at times you have seen the characteristics of our nature; yet, you dive into the folklore of vampires, fallen angels, and a whole host of other fictitious beings to explain us. You have created us as being something we are not. This world is full of ignorant humans that "want-to-be" something they are not and can never be. It has been to your demise. Your very religion cannot discern the fact that we have been and are still a creation beyond you. May I give you an example?"

"We both know that I have no choice but to listen, so do as you please!"

He speaks with words so rapid that the human ear cannot comprehend, but he knows that Rosie understands every word of the song he sings to her. It is a song that would require hours for a human to perform. He begins his own song.

"In your Tablet of Maseth it is written that the children of God *groan within yourselves waiting for the redemption of your body.* Most of you do not understand the very nature of what God has done for you, what he is doing for you and what he must do for you. You mentioned the Garden of Eden not knowing that Adam was truly pronounced as dead: spirit, soul and body. The Greek word *apolutrosis* translates into the word redemption, which means *to ransom fully.* God, through the one you call Jesus, ransomed fully the nature of his chosen ones. He must through a power higher than man is able to comprehend, restore to his beloved humans, a body also."

Rosie is listening to his every word. However, knowing he cannot read her mind, she ponders ways she might separate this creature from his head. If she had known he was coming she would have hidden her large butcher's knife in the thick leaves of the plant she placed near the couch.

The Council Chairman continues, "Now Rosie, something must come forth from the grave that will house the soul and the spirit of man. In Revelation 5:8-9 it is written that the four beasts and four and twenty elders fell down before the Lamb, having every one of them harps, and golden vials full of odors, which are the prayers of saints. And they sung a new song, saying, *Thou art worthy to take the book, and to open the seals thereof: for thou wast slain, and hast redeemed us to God by thy blood out of every kindred, and tongue, and people, and nation.* Most humans know the twenty-four elders represent the redeemed from humanity, even though you argue among yourselves as to what, or who, they are. But the four beasts…you have no idea as to what they are or who they represent. So, you just skip over it and selfishly think of yourselves only. The word beast means a living thing. Something that is non-human, but it does indeed, have a body. A beast that is capable of reproduction. They are not angels, for angels are spirits and have no fleshly body; thus, they cannot reproduce."

He takes a deep breath while waiting to see if Rosie has understood his explanations, and then continues.

"The beasts are the resurrected Nephilim that were slain by Qadar early in creation. They too, someday will stand before the Ancient of Days and sing a new song with the humans that stay faithful unto death. But, don't be deceived, we are as they were. On the other hand, we live for we joined with the Prince of the Air in his rebellion. Are we fallen? Yes, nevertheless, we are able to breed with humans. We were there in the days of Noah, breeding with women to the point that we almost conquered the entire race. Today, we have succeeded, again may I add, in bringing about a day where even the elect of God are nearly all deceived. Oh yes, dearest Rosie, you too will soon give in to the power of the Nephilim. If we can find only one thing that does not come to pass that your God has promised then we will rise victorious over all that he has planned for this Earth. We will be the new rulers of a fallen human race."

"You will never conquer us, Alexander!" Rosie assures him. "Qadar has fallen in every attempt since the Garden, God is sovereign and his word will accomplish that which pleases him and prosper all the things whereto he sends it. Rest assured, the redeemed will sing the new song and you will perish along with Qadar."

Alexander's hatred for the human race cannot be hidden from this woman that sits across the table from him. She recognizes his deceitful plans and will never be misled by them. He doubts for the first time, that he will be able to beguile her.

From the cold realization of his failures, anger flushes the facial features of the Nephilim leader. He reaches beneath his jacket and retrieves several sheets of paper held tightly at the top with a large paper clip and sends them across the table. He tries to laugh, but even for an arrogant Nephilim, it is masked with insecurity. As the sheets slide to the other side of the table, he manages to expel several choice words of profanity punctuated with, "You are a stupid woman Rosie and your ignorance within a short period of time will make you childless as well as a widow!"

Chapter 27

Center Stage

"Whoso diggeth a pit shall fall therein: and he that
rolleth a stone, it will return upon him."
Proverbs 26:27

Full page computer generated photos printed on card stock slide
across the surface of the table. They stop short of falling into her
lap even though she refuses to block their approach. Looking
down, Rosie watches as the sheets connected with a large paper
clip totter on the edge of the table. They bring to memory a time
when her husband and son spent hours playing paper football on an
old table originally owned by her mother. They laughed as they
flipped extra points and field goals between the uprights of their
extended index fingers. It seemed to her they enjoyed the misses
more than the hits. And, as the paper triangles sailed to all parts of
their home, often she discovered that she was the object of those
missiles. Many a paper football was confiscated by her and many
a game was delayed by stormy lectures flowing from her lips.
Both of her men joked and declared their misses were truly
accidental.

"What is this?" she asks pointing at the papers.

The Nephilim leader answers, "Just take a look. You'll see clearly that I mean business and I am a truthful...eh...man!"

She picks up the photos and immediately identifies the top one as the old farm house belonging to Hunter. Unfastening the metal clip at the top, she slaps the first page on the table and nearly faints at the sight of the next photograph. Alexander lets out a roar of hilarity that continues for seconds. As Rosie's alarm becomes more apparent his amusement increases. He knows she is looking at the picture of Calvin lying on Hunter's kitchen floor; covered with blood. Among the protruding broken bones and bruises, she sees deep gashes made by a large knife or sharp sword.

Rosie's body begins to shudder with grief. She weeps with overwhelming sadness as she begins to work her way through Alexander's pictorial account of her husband's death. Working her way through the photos she sees Calvin's body stretched out on a small rail system ready to be rolled into a burning chamber of a crematory. The next sheet shows his body ablaze inside the chamber. She stops for a second to look at the one in which Hunter poses with a grin while bagging cremains into a large white sack.

"You dare pose with a smile? I'll soon wipe it from your face," she swears aloud. The distress on her face cannot mask a new revelation; the Preacher's wife believes she can take the head of both Alexander and Hunter.

"I see hatred in your eyes, my sweetness," whispers Alexander. "Are you not to love your enemies?"

She does not immediately answer the creature across from her but continues to thumb through the photos. There is no denying the next one is Calvin's Harley Davidson motorcycle. Atop the saddle bags is laced a sword. She wishes it was within reach.

Again, she wonders, *Can I make it to the kitchen to retrieve my butcher's knife?*

Another picture portrays her son Dave and his campsite at their hidden cove in the Big South Fork; his custom bike parked nearby. Dave's posture confirms his unawareness of someone secretly taking his picture. She grimaces thinking the next photo will be Dave on the same slab as Calvin, but discovers, it was the last one.

"Where's Davy?" she asks without thinking twice.

"Oh don't worry. As of now he is alive and on his way here to you. However, if you still refuse to become my mate, he will join his father before the day is out. Here, look at these."

He slides her a couple more pictures.

This time, she grabs the photos before they complete their slide. There are only three. The first shows her son riding into a campground. The second one is of him setting up a small tent. The last is a close up of him asleep inside the tent. Looking closer, she discerns not one, but the hilts of two swords partially covered

119

with his baggage. She lays them atop the photos of her husband and with sad eyes, stares at the creature before her.

"Resting peaceful, eh? Those came in only a few minutes ago. If I wanted him dead, he would be. It's up to you. Will he awake from that slumber or not?"

Rosie does not know that Alexander has dispatched one of his daughters along with two other Banah to take the life of her son regardless of her answer. Nevertheless, she will not be defiled by this ancient evil beast that perches in her kitchen like a large vulture sitting on a power pole. She opens her mouth to form words she has been suppressing.

"You vile creature, I pray that God will deliver you into my hands that I might see your blood flow from your worthless body. If not, I hope I can at least see the day of your destruction. Listen to me you monster, I know who you are. I am not blinded by your existence as my husband was, nor do I follow his theology. I know the beasts in the book of Revelation are living creatures. I also know that some will be redeemed and some will dwell in Hell forever...in a resurrected body. For you there will be no redemption! I also know there are other similar beasts in the book, yet they are called venomous, wild animals. You are undoubtedly one of the fallen Nephilim bound for destruction. Yes, I believe there are two classes of Nephilim as there is with mankind, but for the fallen, there is no hope. At least I know this...one day I will see you sink into the pits of hell...your permanent dwelling place.

And I will rejoice! Do not be deceived, there is no escape from the pending judgment and wrath that awaits you and your kind."

He pounds the table once again in the same manner of his arrival.

"What will it be Rosie? Does your little boy Davy live or does he join his father? What's it going to be?"

She wastes no time in delivering her answer, "I will follow God in all that is holy and right. It was never meant for your kind to breed with the daughters of men. You left your domain in rebellion, but I will not. I serve a God that will have his way and into his hands have I delivered my son. Nothing in this world, including you, can separate me from the love of God. The answer has not changed. It is the same…NEVER!"

Chapter 28

The Morning After

"A lying tongue hateth those that are afflicted by
it; and a flattering mouth worketh ruin."
Proverbs 26:28

There is an existence of urgency in the course of action he plans for the day. Overriding it is a need for caution; thus, he proceeds with the task that lies before him with silence combined with stealth-like movements. This process has been acquired through many years of training during his military career. He pauses briefly to recall the operating procedures of the loading ramp in the rear of the motor home. He gives thanks, to some force or concept of deity that he knows not, that somewhere in the passion of the night, the wild, flaming-haired woman had with pride revealed it to him.

He rolls his motorcycle to the back of the motor home, which he calls a coach, and decides loading it will be the last thing he does. The grinding gears of the ramp last night, he remembers, had drawn attention from the nearby RV's. First, he will stow his gear along with the swords he took from Hunter. Those, he decides, will be stored behind the passenger seat for quick and ready availability. Len's body was already wrapped securely in large garbage bags he found in the cabinets. He continues to whisper appreciation that there had been little blood. The beating death she suffered resulted in massive bruises which had swollen and closed the wounds inflicted from the broken glass. A roll of camouflage duct tape, which he never left home without, was used to secure the plastics bags. Afterward, he folded her body inside his small pup tent, wrapping it with cords to give it an appearance of a larger tent. Then he placed it in the front of the storage area where he knew he would be able to squeeze the bike in diagonally. There was still room in the opposite corner to place anything else he might need to store.

As he rolls the bike from the camp site to the back of the coach, he feels the dew soaked grass under his feet. Looking back to the east, he sees the first hint of light pushing to erase the darkness of the night. Soon, the sun will reclaim this land he treads. He must hurry, for he desires to escape in the shadows of the night.

"Do you need help with that thing?"

Dave is shocked by the voice that penetrates a darkness that emerged victorious after the full moon disappeared into a land of its own. He stops to flash his small military light in the direction of the voice. The surreal illumination of the red lens enhances the crimson sight before him. A young man has ceased the disconnection of his own motor home to engage Dave in conversation.

Curly red hair frames the square contours of his jaws. His ruddy skin is highlighted with muscular features, accented from the glowing light in Dave's hand. If the man's voice stunned him, the vision before him erases all shock and replaces it with genuine fear. This man could pass as a twin to the woman of the night that he had just slain. Somewhere in the depths of his mind, his years of lying and deceit will serve as his rescue; the traits of a liar which his mother observed in him at an early age. A quick chain of flowing lies would spew forth from his mouth like a river of contempt for any who challenged him. He moved from one lie to another never concerned about the poison and treachery they bred.

"No thanks," is his only answer as he turns to ease his bike along the grass.

"What's the hurry?" the voice asks.

Dave knows from the proximity of the question that the young man has followed him.

"I'm almost finished. All I have to do is load up the bike and I'll be on my way."

The visitor shows no signs of a quick departure and stands boldly facing the light from Dave flashlight which is shining, once again, in his eyes. His bright green irises are blurred from the fiery red haze of the Dave's light. Together, they present the young man as a demonic apparition.

"Where's that beautiful woman I saw you with last night?" he asks.

"That's my wife if it's any concern of yours. I'm letting her sleep in so she can drive later today. We have a long haul planned for the day, so if you don't mind, I'll get on with my business and you can attend to yours. There are others around us that would like to sleep. I'm moving quietly, so I don't wake them and if you have any consideration at all for others, you'll do likewise."

Fiendish or not, Dave has grown tired of the nosy prying human and concludes that he had lusting eyes for the previous owner of his newly acquired coach.

The young man grunts defiantly but turns to leave. The audible words are sufficient in volume for Dave, but the language is strange. A language this world traveling soldier had never heard. He ponders the origin while glancing back to ensure the young man is indeed departing. Dave directs his flashlight toward the adjacent motor home to assist the stranger in his departure. The urgency in the young man's preparation compels Dave to get his bike loaded and get on the road.

It only takes minutes for him to lower the platform and roll the bike on it. There he secures it with ratchet straps before hopping to the upper level to pull the lever to raise the ramp. As he walks through the coach to start the next stage of his journey to Copper Town, he notices the young man next door has nearly finished all his work and seems to be determined to pull out from the campground with him.

Dave pulls out and notices the driver to the other side of his site is also preparing to pull out. He works his way with great care to the entrance of I-40 and rapidly accelerates to the speed limit. He sets the cruise accordingly while declaring that with daylight he will drive faster. But for now, he will be careful to have no accident or draw attention to his coach. The dead body inside could prove a most difficult task to explain even for the master of deceit.

Traveling westward, he knows the young man will follow. He swears under his breath that he will put as many miles between them as possible.

Dave does not know that the distance of separation he desires is not from one of his former campsite neighbors, but from two.

Chapter 29

The Silver Helmet

"Boast not thyself of to morrow; for thou knowest
not what a day may bring forth."
Proverbs 27:1

"Rachel! Oh my darling Rachel! Where are you?"

The little man twists his hands in agony. He rubs one
almost raw and realizing what he has done, he ceases. Within
minutes the hands are exchanged and the other is rubbed near
bloody. Somewhere in the depths of his mind a thought begins to
form…and then as quickly, it fades away. Like the chalk boards
his teacher often allowed him to clean, his mind is cleansed
again…and again. On the fresh board there are no formulas, no
assignments, no names of students who would stay in at break, no
chalk dust to cause his eyes to water and his lungs to swell with
coughs; now, there is nothing…only a void. But there he discovers
his Rachel and calls pleadingly to her, "Rachel!"

His eyes dart nervously from left to right seeking to claim
some hint of reality, or is it sanity, in a desire to recognize his
environment.

The wooden pallets he laboriously carried up the northern slopes are placed meticulously beneath the uppermost cliff ledges. Rope, string and wire were methodically woven together and united to form the unmistakable boundary of his domain. Within the perimeter, a conglomerate of roadside collectables is set in an orderly arrangement making them most beneficial in the place he calls home. At times, it escapes his care and the dirt walkway to the entry becomes blocked with avalanches of collectables piled from confused thoughts and lapses of memory. Yet, in the midst of it all, in time or by some supernatural guidance, he awakes in the large downy sleeping bag he calls his bed. The canvas sides and top of his shelter are new and surprisingly in good condition; considering they were castaways.

Sometimes, he is amazed by the quality and quantity of food left for him at various places of his wanderings. Other times, he is just as pleased with the food he shares in the cool shade with several of his canine friends. But tonight, he searches the depths of his consciousness for memories of Rachel and calls her name again, "RACHEL?"

"Home Sweet Home," he declares while turning to look for the sign he painted and placed over the shanty. Then, he remembers that it was not painted, he found it in a garbage can behind the casino. That thought, too, is completely erased for he remembers the sign was given him by a store owner. He surrenders to frustration for he cannot visualize the wall upon which it was placed. The past fades as the present rushes forth to shift his focus to search for a picture of Rachel. There is none to be found.

For assistance, he pleads with his surroundings.

"Where's the picture? I must have it for as hard as I try, I cannot remember what her sweet face looks like! Rachel, where's your picture?"

For a brief space in time, his mind clears to show him that all his efforts are thwarted for he is standing idle. That too fades into darkness as his mind becomes vacant. Like a zombie, he drifts to the edge of the cliff to cast his eyes down on the little town. It glows in the darkness of night. The brilliance of its lights at the foot of his mountain is like gold sparkling in the moonlight. He grabs an old rifle scope that will allow him to see into the busy streets which are being swallowed by the flickering neon lights of the large casino. A vision invades the vacancy. It is a vision of a vampire with fangs as long as his finger and a body as tall as a tree. He trembles with fear while his heart thumps against his chest; he holds his breath near the point of fainting. That fear, to his relief, fades but is replaced with an emerging dread for the approaching night. For a brief second, he knows sleep will not come.

As the dread fades, so does the vision of the giant vampire. Adjusting the zoom on his scope, he gazes down into the town; for what reason he cannot explain. His mind is blank...once again!

Taking off his large western hat, he wipes sweat from his forehead. He recalls the hat was given to him as a gift from Alexander. Or, had it been from Alexander's friend Giles? There is not an answer for he forgets the question when he glances into the sweaty liner of his hat.

"What is this?" he asks himself when he observes the liner. It is covered with aluminum foil.

He tries to recall why the thickly layered foil is inside his hat. He stops his mad pacing to think about it.

"Does it serve as some reminder that I should not remove it? Or is it there by design? Maybe…Rachel gave it to me or decorated my hat with it? It does shine and sparkle. That looks like something she would do."

He yells down into the streets that are too far away to hear him, "Rachel, are you coming home tonight?"

Replacing the hat, he remembers the vision of the vampire creature; fortunately, that too, fades. Thus spins the endless pattern of his thoughts. Not to his disappointment, for every time he returns to a place of his revolving memories, there is freshness as if it was the first time it invaded his mind.

Tonight, he once again thinks of Rachel. If his mind would allow, he would give thanks that tonight he is free from another fear he has; a fear that aliens invaded Earth and were seeking to destroy him before he could reveal their existence. Some night, or day in the future, he would remember them again. But for the remainder of this night and before sleep overtakes him with dreams he will fail to remember, his thoughts are of Rachel.

Again he cries out, "Rachel, don't worry you have a guardian angel with you…and so do I!"

His words are not unheard. Above him standing in the brilliance of an almost full moon stands the Nephilim, Giles, with arms folded. From atop the outcropping rocky ledge, his fixed stare is upon the camp and the little man dwelling there. With pride and defiance he stands in his full created form. It is night, the time he is permitted to enjoy and relish in the fact that he does not have to mask himself with the distasteful human form. The camp below is one he visits often. Protection of the little man dwelling there has been assigned to him by the leader of the clan. Dan was the little man's name. The Nephilim jovially referred to him as "Dan the Man". How fitting the title is.

Giles squats. Although he stands near sixteen feet in height, from his kneeling perch on the edge of the cliff, with wings folded, he appears as a harmless tiny sparrow. Harmless he is not. Within him rages an ancient thirst for blood; especially, human blood. Over the years, he and the other Nephilim have been successful in satisfying this hunger with the blood of animals. Cattle, sheep and horses were specifically bred and maintained to meet the constant demands of their insatiable desires. Some of the Nephilim kept companion canine pets to fulfill the hunger. Their pets meet the need on a small and whimsical scale. Humans would probably call them *snacks*.

But tonight, Giles defiantly glares at Dan with contempt because Alexander has placed unnecessary restrictions upon the clan. A restriction that they must refrain from taking human blood; the blood he desires. The brightening rays from the moon as it reaches its full glory, fuels his desire to kill this human and consume his blood. Giles, along with the other Nephilim, are to the point that they are ready to pay the penalty of isolation into the Garden for healing. Perhaps the return to hiding in dark, isolated areas during the day was well worth the nightly supply of fresh human blood. He would not be able to assume the human form to walk in the sun for several days after consuming human blood; but he was ready for the old paths. Besides, he hated living in a human form, even if it was for daylight hours only.

Alexander rescued this idiot of a human from Rachel, a little town in Nevada located midway along the ninety miles of Route 375 known as the Extraterrestrial Highway. While hitch-hiking through the area, Dan imagined he met up with aliens. It had been quite comical to watch this little vagabond. He dressed in army fatigues, which he thought hid him among a few trees and bushes near the rest area, while spying on the Nephilim operations. At the rest stop, he begged food from tourists and startled them with his wild tales of encounters with aliens. Even if he could have possibly gone undetected in his hiding places, the glow of aluminum foil wrapped around his head would have revealed him. The foil prevented the aliens from reading his thoughts, so he claimed. Thus, they did not know he was aware of their plans to invade the world.

Alexander was intrigued with the fact that Dan's thoughts could not be discerned by the Nephilim; thus, he wanted to keep him alive for observation. Giles knew the reason for their failures to read his mind. Dan was a fool who had few thoughts and those he had were not worth knowing. Yet, their constant attempts to read his confused thoughts yielded nothing.

Perhaps Slim was to blame for Dan's mental instability. Thinking it a comical thing to do, he picked Dan up in flight one night and dropped him deep within Area 51; an area operated by the Nephilim and considered to be one of top secrecy by the country's government. There, under Nephilim leadership, they worked with human allies to successfully collect the ninth sword of the ten formed by the Ancient of Days. These swords were to be given to a Maseth warrior, called a Bachar, who could use it to destroy renegade Nephilim clans. One sword forged for each of the ten clans.

Dan wandered in at the Nephilim celebration of finding the ninth one. Rather than killing him, Alexander found him amusing and brought him, along with the sword, to Copper Town.

"He will serve in demonstrating to people that we are a normal American town. We too, will have a street person. Giles, it will be up to you to make sure nothing happens to him. Besides, there is something about this one I have not encountered before. We need to keep an eye on him and observe all that he does."

"What a waste of time," grumbles Giles.

Settling into his nightly perch, the Nephilim relaxes his muscles and desires to consume Dan's blood. For now, he will share the view of the town with Dan the Man. He needs no magnification to observe the depths of the streets; sadly, he sees them only with brilliant shades of gray even though the silvery light of the moon surrounds him.

Chapter 30

Revelations of Ideology

"Let another man praise thee, and not thine own mouth; a stranger, and not thine own lips."
Proverbs 27:2

Often throughout the long years of his life, he weighed the worth of existence. Hopeless visions of *what had been* intertwined with *what was* emerged with a rapture of despair in the hopelessness of *what will be*! He had come to believe that his past and his present left him with only a faint hope that his kind might survive. Unexpectedly, his depression had been eased to some degree by the woman sitting across the table from him. She captured his heart the first time he laid eyes on her. No other human ever penetrated the depths of his soul to stir the embers of an emotion he thought was lost…love. But this one resurrected it like a mountain spring gushing upward from the earth with bright sparkling drops of freshness.

He closed his eyes at times to listen to her laughter when she and her husband had no idea anyone was near. The sound of her voice was destined to echo forever in his mind. The silliness he once thought love to be is now replaced with a longing for what he fully understood it was. Her voice rang with beauty as desirable as the songs of his kind before they fell from the grace of the Ancient One. The warmth of love growing once again in his darkened heart makes him think the colors of the rainbow can become visible again. Sadly, upon opening his eyes, he glares at the grays he has been cursed to see throughout eternity. Still, he longs to take this woman as his mate. He made that desire known amongst the Nephilim by branding her with the Mark of the Yada.

She sits glaring at him with hatred. He can only hope that in time her disgust will transform to esteem; especially, when she experiences the touch of his hands upon her body. That first touch would tax the virtue of his essence, but would bestow power upon her she could never envision. The power given him in creation is something humans cannot obtain, but he desired to bless her with it. Once she experienced it, she would rise above the weaknesses of humanity. If only she would willingly accept the offer to become his mate, she would become the most powerful and feared woman on the planet. Nevertheless, this beautiful creature would soon be his...with, or without, her consent.

"Well Rosie, do as you please. Soon I will have all ten swords forged by the Ancient One and there will be no stopping me. Your son is on his way here with the only two remaining. One of those swords was loaned to John Calvin to determine if he was Bachar. Obviously, he was not. I am not sure yet for whom the last two have been forged, but when I combine them in the circle of life at the new moon, their power will be transferred to me. I alone will own and control them all."

The woman he desires so intimately sits and continues to stare at him with growing disgust. He has no idea that what he thinks he is making known has already been revealed to her by the Ancient of Days.

On the other hand, she will not relinquish the vast knowledge of him and his clan that she has been given; nor will she share secrets of the swords that only she understands. That will be her surprise! When the time comes, that knowledge will serve as the downfall of the hellish creature sitting across from her.

"All right, my lady, hear me plainly. Your son is on his way here and should arrive within two days...at the peak of the full moon. That is, he shall arrive if your answer pleases me. Regardless, it will be my decision if he lives or if he dies."

Alexander does not reveal to her that two previous attempts to take her son's life by the hands of Banah have failed. The Nephilim clans have expressed their dissatisfaction with the leader and are demanding permission to take this matter into their own hands. No human could possibly defeat a Banah, let alone two of them within two days. Alexander insisted they must observe her son to see from what source he draws such power. The evil deeds of his past certainly do not ascertain he is Maseth, nor is he one of theirs, yet his power cannot be explained. It could be disastrous for a Nephilim to place himself in jeopardy. As much as he loves his offspring, he is willing to continue to sacrifice their lives in order to study this renegade human.

"Alexander, I have told you that my son's life is not in your hands. You can do nothing to him unless God allows it. I trust in him and him alone."

The Nephilim leader tires of the religious nonsense which this woman continues to prattle. He makes his final declaration.

"You are no longer restricted to your home. The town is at your pleasure. Enjoy it! Run, jog, exercise; do as you please but remember that you do NOT have liberty to leave. There will always be someone over your shoulder to watch you, protect you and to make sure you do not try to leave. If you change your mind and want to see your son alive, you know where I will be."

Rosie spits at the Nephilim sitting across the table and watches as the spittle splatters across his face. This time, her actions bring forth the anger she intended.

Alexander leaps from his chair. As the leader of the great Clan Shachar, he will no longer be insulted by this weak human even though he has fallen deeply in love with her. He pounds both fists into the table top and observes cracks springing forth along the seams of the boards once held by glue. He grabs the kitchen chair he sat in and whirls it against the large portal door. It crashes with such force that only splinters fall across the floor. Protected from direct sunlight, his physical features change from that of Alexander the human, to that of Alexander the majestic Nephilim leader.

When he yanks the portal door open, the massive portal moans from the force exerted upon its thick fixtures of wooden beams, but it refuses to be denied its purpose of separating the Garden of the Nephilim from the world beyond. With no further comments, Alexander disappears through the portal. It closes spontaneously on ancient hinges like a stone being rolled across the entry of a tomb.

Rosie sees the analogy and prays that the closing of the door foreshadows the downfall of this creature and not the end of mankind. She had no glimpse of the room behind the door, but realizes that her future, and that of her son, is as bleak as the world beyond the portal.

Chapter 31

A Brother's Wrath

"A stone is heavy, and the sand weighty; but a
fool's wrath is heavier than them both."
Proverbs 27:3

"Rostislav, where are you?"

The speaker on his phone blasts out with the voice of his
dad.

Rostislav, nicked named Rosti by Alexander answers, "I'm
on I-40 West, Father. We are near Holbrook, Arizona. Illarion is
behind me, but we have not caught up with him yet."

Alexander's large fingers struggle with the little cell phone.
Continuing to hold it in front of his monstrous teeth, he sits
perched on the roof of his home glaring down into the little town
of Nevada that will soon be the capitol of his new world empire.

"Son," he continues, "you lost him. He is no longer on I-
40. I just received an update that he is camped at the Mesa Verde

National Monument in Colorado. He has an overnight rental, so he'll probably be on his way bright and early tomorrow morning."

"Father, I can double back and be there after midnight."

"No, you know what that means by him taking that route, do you not?"

Rosti answers immediately, "Yes, Dad. It means he plans to come in on U.S. 50. But, I'll make sure he never gets there."

When Alexander uses Rosti instead of Rostislav, his son always responds with Dad instead of Father. The latter name was used in business and formalities but the former was used by Alexander in personal and confidential father-to-son conversations. Alexander was giving instructions to his son in a fatherly fashion rather than with Nephilim assertiveness.

"No, Rosti! Your mission has been changed. I want you to send Illarion directly through Las Vegas to Copper Town. He is to relieve his father in watching over Dan. I need Giles to help with final preparations here before Qadar arrives."

"Dad, you know what he did to Len! Please let me be the one to avenge her. My heart aches from being separated from her. Since birth, we have not only lived as brother and sister, but as best friends. Dad, my heart is broken. I can take this man down, I know I can. I am much stronger than my sister."

"Rostislav…the answer is NO! I want him alive. You now must make sure nothing happens to him on his journey here. This one, I want for myself. I will no longer risk the lives of my children. Now, work your way up to the intersection of I-15 and

US-50. Get some sleep and wait for him to come through. Do not let him know you are tailing him. Do you understand?"

"Yes Father, I understand."

"Okay, keep a little distance between you. You will not need to keep him in sight. I'll have plenty of reports coming directly to you the minute he hits Highway 50. Just take care son and I promise you there will be atoning blood for that of your sister's."

"That's all that I need to hear Father, but I hope that you change your mind and let me have him. Nevertheless, it is not my will but your will I seek, Dad."

Chapter 32

Looking over the Edge

"Wrath is cruel, and anger is outrageous; but who
is able to stand before envy?"
Proverbs 27:4

Outstretched hands reach to grasp the large orb glowing in the darkness of the night. With palms facing forward, the hands hesitate with indecisiveness as to what object they are to capture. Will it be the silvery moon, or is it part of the ancient Anasazi ruins below?

Dave's secret ascent, a forbidden one, has empowered him with pleasure. The adrenaline from his defiance flows through his body in perfect harmony with a quickened pulse. It was a laborious climb up the cliff walls, but he finally stands victorious at the summit. The ecstasy of his accomplishment serves, momentarily, as a means of clearing his head. During the long drive here today, he must have pondered a thousand thoughts; along with as many plans of action. He camped at the park's recreational area and hiked cross country to get here undetected by park officials. His original plan was to carry Len's carefully wrapped body up the slope and toss it over in an effort to make it look as if she had fallen accidentally. Somewhere along the journey, he ditched that plan replacing it with a better one. One more worthy of his talents and one he will complete tomorrow night.

He whispers softly into the night, "one more day, my dear, and then I will take care of your final arrangements."

He calmly laughs standing with arms outstretched to the heavens like a pagan god inviting the world to come, fall down before him and worship.

Folding his arms, he crosses his legs and lowers himself to a sitting position atop the rocky surface of the cliff dwellings. Knowing the moon will be full in all its glory within two days, he wishes he could linger in this place until then. There is so much before him he wants to explore in the lightness of day.

Dave originally planned to drive nonstop through Las Vegas to Copper Town in his effort to find his mother. But, he had changed his mind on the road today believing the two men he encountered in Oklahoma City were hot on his heels. He made this detour with confidence to throw them off his trail. Tomorrow, he would sleep in and get plenty of rest before completing the final part of his journey. If all goes well, he will drive across Utah tomorrow, pick up Highway 50 and work his way into the mountainous area of Nevada. There he will dispose of the rotting corpse, but tonight he will rest in the comfort of the large and spacious bed near the rear of his new coach.

For a moment, Dave sits wondering about the Anasazi Indians that had deserted several of their dwellings in this area. Here in the Mesa Verde National Monument, a half-million gallon reservoir had been excavated by them. In Chaco Cultural National Historic Park in New Mexico they had abandoned a five-story pueblo "apartment house" that contained 800 rooms. Years ago, he had ridden his bike across country and stopped at the Aztec Ruins in New Mexico where he observed a huge sunken kiva that had been covered with a 95-ton roof supported only by four wooden posts.

"Where did you go?" He asks. His words are whispered for he knows park rangers could be below him somewhere in the darkness. If he was detected by them, there was little chance he could escape into the night as the Anasazi had.

"Some say you never left," he begins his lecture to the stones and departed spirits that remain near the site.

"The present-day Indian tribes in the area claim they can trace their ancestry to the Anasazi clan. Strong scientific evidence seems to confirm that the Ancient Ones did not disappear mysteriously, but evacuated the major cultural centers like Chaco, Mesa Verde and Kayenta over centuries ago. They joined with what people now know as the Hopi and Zuni clans in Arizona and New Mexico. There is evidence they spread to many other Pueblo villages along the Río Grande."

As if pausing to give students a chance to finish their notes and gather their thoughts, he sits motionless before challenging them with the next question.

"But we should ask ourselves this: Why did they depart?"

Dave's pause is intentional to allow him time to review the colorful literature he gathered earlier today while touring the site. Bored, he ends his lecture by defiantly littering the area below him with his collection of pamphlets. Slowly, he stands with a smirking grin and stretches his arm upward to the moon for one last time. He yawns and looks over the edge of the cliff. Then he springs over the ledge like a panther and with ease, rapidly makes his decent.

In the darkness of the night, he like the Anasazi disappears.

Chapter 33

Retracing Steps

"Open rebuke is better than secret love."
Proverbs 27:5

A flooding of fresh mountain air fills her lungs and invigorates her pace. Long black legs stretch visibly before her. Although slender, they are well toned and muscular. Once she reaches the pace she desires, she settles in to maintain it for the remainder of her run. Somewhere along her predetermined path, she may enhance it again; but, she is determined not to slow until her run is over. Today, in the mid-morning hours, she retraces the tracks of her disastrous night run a few weeks ago.

She surveys people along the street who waved to her on previous runs and called out greetings accompanied by smiles. Now, with condescension, they turn away. The whole town seems to be assigned the burdensome task of watching every step she makes. For a brief second, she sniggers defiantly and thinks about breaking into a dead run out of town westward along US 50. She visualizes a large army of humans, and non-humans, running after her like a scene in a sci-fi movie she once watched. She stimulates her imagination as another giggle slips through her lips.

"Yeah," she shouts to everyone.

"Zombies may have chased the heroine out of town, but she returned and killed them all. Likewise, I will have my day!"

She waves at a few tourists that smile and wave back. Some of the women scold their husbands when they are caught gawking lustfully at her body. They find it difficult not to stare for her tight running shorts and sports bra reveal the perfection of feminine features.

It sickens her that some men are so perverted for her clothes are appropriate for the sport she loves so much.

Crossing Main Street, she heads into the depths of the dreaded campgrounds. A new manager stands in the door of the welcoming center. However, his glare of pure hatred matches or exceeds that of the previous one. The campground is near full, unlike the night of her run when only a few campers were in the lower area. In seconds, her heart pounds with vigor as she catches a 'second wind' which will assist her in maintaining the grueling pace up the hillside into the tent sites.

Events of that run, suppressed into forgetfulness, now return to companion those she remembers. Together, they flood her subconscious revealing every detail of the tragic incident. Directly to her left is the camp site where the bikers drug her to execute their sinful and heinous deeds; folly seeded deep within their dark souls. It was here she recalls that human life was taken.

She was responsible for one of them and somewhere in the roots of her thoughts, she acknowledges, "If Alexander had not arrived when he did, I would have killed all three of them!"

She waves at a young boy standing at the back of a Saturn SUV wearing a cochlear implant behind his left ear. What he may lack in auditory perception has served to heighten acuity of his other senses. He has watched her intently, and with interest, since she crossed the road and made her way upward toward his camp. A big smile covers his face as he extends to her a sincere wave of welcome. The wave makes her feel that he would love for her to stop and visit with him.

Rosie smiles, returns a wave and looks deep into his brown eyes which sparkle with delight; and illustrate, perhaps, a slight sign of innocent mischief. He laughs while continuously waving.

The boy's parents are busy making a late breakfast while his teenage sister sits completely oblivious to Rosie's presence. Miles and days have separated her from her friends; thus, her tiny thumbs hammer tirelessly on the keypads of her cell phone in hopes of discovering all that she has missed since her departure.

In the campsite to her right, a lady stands with hands on her hips. Her family finished breakfast hours ago and is packing the last of their gear to make a departure that Rosie knows to be *late*. The husband bears the resemblance of being in the military for he jumps at her every command. Their teenage son, sporting hair below his shoulders, walks about mumbling words that no one can hear. Rosie does not know that his backpack is laden with the latest electronic gadgets and books that will soon be arranged across the back seat of their small car. From there, he will tune out his parents, along with any attempts they make to communicate, and enter into a realm of his own; a realm in which he rules supreme.

Rosie detects the young man is not overly thrilled at being forced away from the comfort of his home. He looks at her briefly, but does not wave. He is too deep in thought for casual conversation and paces back and forth like a caged tiger.

Rosie leaves both families behind in the campground and crests the top of the hill to turn left along the graveled road. Within minutes, she nears the Estate of Alexander. Her last vision of his home included two Mastiffs sitting like statues inside the cast iron gates. She is not surprised to discover they are still there; just as she had left them. For a second, she is startled by a figure standing beyond the dogs. Grudgingly, she decides to stop to comply with the beckoning of Kara, the Banah daughter of Alexander.

"Good morning Rosie! It is so good to see you running along this old road again. How do you feel?"

Rosie searches for a reply, in hopes of only returning the salutation. After a slight hesitation, she answers, "Good morning to you too Kara. I'm feeling great thank you. How are you feeling?"

"Never better, how about coming in for a glass of tea?"

"No thanks. With nothing else to do, I have decided to get back to my running…thought about making a couple of laps this morning."

Kara steps toward the gate and unlatches it.

"Oh, come on in for a few minutes and then you can run to your heart's content. Dad's in Reno for the day and I'd like to show you something. I'd also like to catch you up with Dave's progress. He's on his way here you know."

Rosie knows there will be no denying this woman; besides, her mention of Dave meant there was more here than meets the eye. Her running would wait. She will hear what this woman has to say.

"Okay, since you insist. But, if you don't mind, I'll pass on the tea. I don't want to eat or drink anything until I finish my running."

Kara giggles for she knows the real reason Rosie does not desire food or drink from her hands. Like her father, today she will lay her cards on the table.

"Rosie, don't you know that if Dad, or I, wanted to poison you, we would have already done it. Dad wants you alive and he has charged the whole town with that responsibility. So…eat, drink and be merry!"

There is no response from the woman entering into the home of Alexander. She simply follows with a new pace motivated by intrigue and inquiry, rather than from obedience.

Chapter 34

A Labyrinth of Technology

"Faithful are the wounds of a friend; but the kisses
of an enemy are deceitful."
Proverbs 27:6

Alexander's dogs trot ahead to assume guardian stances beside the double door entry of his colossal mountain chalet. They have secured the route for Kara and now sit watching intently to ensure she is not followed. When she opens the door, they rush inside and take up similar poses beside the tall doors located to the right of the foyer. They were trained years ago for this act of faithful servitude to their Master and never cease to perform it.

Unknown to Rosie, Kara is dressed in the robe she wore in her temptation of John Calvin. While walking up the drive, she loosened the sash tied tightly to her waist which served only to showcase her hour glass figure. Now, the dangling silk rope slips to the sides to reveal lustrous feminine features that were concealed seconds ago.

Kara is not shy. She permits her robe to open wide while maneuvering to open the large doors. The purpose is served for her breasts are freed from the confinement of the robe. With a small step toward the door, she grabs the massive knob with her left hand allowing her elbow to drop downward at a sharp angle. She floats her right elbow downward in the same position and turns to face the Preacher's wife. As a result, her robe slides from her shoulders and comes to rest in the crooks of her arms. With her body now completely exposed to Rosie, she releases the door knob and extends both arms to Rosie with an invitation to embrace.

"Is there anything I can do for you before we look in Dad's study?"

Kara cares not what Rosie's answer will be. *Nothing ventured...nothing gained* was her motto and today she is yearning for a few hours of pleasure with this beautiful woman.

There is no hesitation, nor shame, as Rosie slowly examines Kara's skin as if seeking to discover some flaw. She does not. Satisfied this Banah has no scars marking her for Nephilim breeding, she turns her head away. She is not tempted by this woman. Nor would she have been if Kara's handsome brother, Rosti, had stood before her naked. She had been faithful to her husband since marriage and faithful to her God long before.

Somewhere in the files of physiological observations, it escapes both women that their bodies are proportionally the same in all aspects but one. The Banah stands exposed as a beautiful perfection of snowy white. The light clothing of Rosie's running attire does not hide her femininity. Although they are soaked with the same fluids covering her body, she glistens and shines with a perfection of blackness.

The Banah laughs, "I guess not! You're stronger than John Calvin. You don't know it, but I tempted him likewise. He didn't completely surrender to me either, but I did get a kiss from him. Your old man was not a bad kisser…for a preacher!"

She laughs again, observing the face of Calvin's wife. She detects no hint of emotion from her; thus, she abandons her attempts of seduction. Kara pulls her robe together and turns to open the door to her father's study. Her guardians enter ahead of her and resume the familiar statue-like poses inside the door. From there, they will deny entry, or exit, to anyone unless it is granted by Alexander or his daughter.

Upon entering, Rosie displays the first hint of emotions. It is one of amazement. Several monitors, larger than she knew existed, cover the walls of the Clan Leader's study. Smaller ones, but still larger than any television she and Calvin had owned, are situated on shelves behind his desk. Others are placed strategically atop the large desk and on the counters surrounding it. A collection of swords are displayed in a semi-circle on the back wall. The rainbow of weapons is shortened on the right side by empty spaces allocated for two swords that are missing.

"This is what I wanted to show you Rosie…honestly…it really is!"

Rosie nods with an answer slowly looking around the room. "Wow! What is all this stuff?"

"It's the center of the Nephilim Empire. This is where Dad works and corresponds with the other clans. They have been responsible for the vast human development of technology in the last thirty years or so. Men of their choosing have gotten rich developing a means for them to communicate on a global web."

"Here, look at this one," she continues pointing towards the largest screen which was mounted on the wall to the right of the entry. It was a position that made it easily visible from Alexander's desk. Rosie recognizes that soft lights against a black background serve as a two dimensional illustration of Earth. She quickly discerns the boundary lines of countries, cities and other geographical features labeled with neon colors. Large blue and red splashes fill the globe and are intermingled with smaller ones. While the smaller blink, the larger submissively fade in and out; both in endless repetition. Much of the earthly activity represented on the monitor was understood only by the Nephilim. Unknown to the women, a great deal was interpreted by the Leader of Shachar and him alone.

Kara continues. "This one displays satellite imagery developed by the Nephilim. They have not shared this with humans. It registers thermal energy emitted by Nephilim and Maseth activity. The large red sections represent the locations of each remaining clan. You can see that only three clans are still in existence: one here in Nevada, one in Spain and one in China. The smaller red dots are few, but they serve to keep up with individual Nephilim while they are traveling outside clan territory."

"What are the blue colors?" Rosie asks.

"They show energy readings of the Maseth. When I was younger, there was a lot of blue on this screen, but now they are rapidly disappearing. Seems mankind's need for a God and to have faith in one is almost gone. But, look at the smaller screen on the other side of the door."

Yes, Rosie thinks, *it's smaller but it's still larger than anything I've ever seen*!

Alexander's daughter notices the awestruck eyes of the preacher's wife and delights in her knowledge of the Nephilim Kingdom. She is eager to continue her theatrical seminar.

"Notice the bright blue clusters? As I was saying, the blue symbolizes Maseth activity. The smaller circles, only three up there, are individual Maseth known as Bachar. Those dots alert the Nephilim that a Bachar has been called forth by the Old One to retrieve his sword. In the past, the Bachar always emerged close to the clan he was chosen to destroy. But look! There are only three and they are all here in Copper Town. Needless to say, that has really created some concern among the Nephilim clans."

Kara pauses for a second, showing she too feels helpless gazing at the light show upon both screens. She blinks, shakes her head and turns to face her dark skinned companion before resuming her story.

156

Rosie scratches her head. This unconscious act will assist her in comprehending the depths of this Nephilim secrecy.

"Okay, I see, but what about the bright yellow ones on the screen?"

"Those represent the locations of the Swords of the Bachar. This is how Dad found the final three swords. Amazing is it not? They were supposed to be close to the clan for which each was created, but puzzling enough, two of the last three were not. Dad was able to isolate the locations of each remaining sword within a 50 mile radius. It has taken years to find the one in Riley and one in Nevada. The one in Campeche, Mexico was discovered by accident by an archeologist working down there a few years ago. The money Dad gave him far surpassed the fame he would have received by publishing his discovery."

"But also notice that there are only two glowing circles of yellow. One glows exceedingly bright in this area of Nevada because Dad has eight of the original swords on exhibit behind his desk. The other one is moving westward toward us and soon…the two will merge. That circle represents your son Dave. He has both missing swords and when he arrives, Dad's collection will be complete."

Rosie is eager to ask her question, "Can you tell me more about the swords?"

"The swords," Kara purrs like a puma. "Oh yes, the swords…indeed I can tell you more about the swords. After all, that's why you are here!

Chapter 35

The Mountain Pass

"The full soul loatheth an honeycomb; but to the
hungry soul every bitter thing is sweet."
Proverbs 27:7

Tomorrow night he will celebrate in the glory of a full moon. The
promise of an unclouded night will find him basking in silvery rays
of grandeur.

Long and slow has been his journey over Highway 50 but
he will arrive in Copper Town on time. The trip was slow simply
because he sought to be here late at night

Presently, he sits overlooking the canyon near Connors
Pass in Nevada. It is the time of night when the loneliest highway
in the nation becomes its loneliest. At this particular place and this
particular time, rarely will a headlight pierce the isolated expanse
through Schell Creek.

Earlier, he crested the top of the mountain range at an
elevation of 7,722 feet and descended to the pullover which was
nearly a half mile above his position. From there, the view had
been nearly as magnificent as it would have been in the day.

Single-leaf pinion and juniper trees decorated the terrain reminding him of Christmas since they appear to be decorated with silvery tinsel. Somewhere in the dark desert below and several miles to the west, the little town of Ely had closed for the night; only a few street lights marked its presence along route 50.

From his observation point, both he and his bike are undetected by any driver that might foolishly venture along this highway so late at night. Sitting down, he makes himself comfortable by leaning against a large boulder. Once comfortable, he easily monitors the fire below the pull-off viewing area above him. It rages with tall flames casting eerie red glows downward into the canyon where he sits. The fiery colors against the silvery moonlight please him. With large binoculars, he zooms in to witness the details of the fire he ignited. He thinks of the plans he laid that day and seeks to discover anything that might have escaped his attention. In so doing, he retraces his route.

During the day, he had lingered at restaurants, rest areas and a gas station near the state line in an effort to bring to fruition his labors. He topped off with diesel in Utah. It was there too, that he filled a five gallon can with fuel and set it behind the driver's seat. The fumes from the can were almost unbearable during his drive through the Great Basin National Park up to Major's Place.

Late into the night, he drove downward toward Cave Lake where he knew the pullover would serve to accomplish his mission. There, the two lane road surrendered its guardrail system at the lower side of the gravel parking area. Long ago a run-away truck had taken that portion of the guardrails with it on a downward drop into the gorge. To his benefit, it was never replaced.

Once there, Dave wasted no time. He retrieved Len's body and placed it behind the steering wheel. The entire can of diesel was splashed around the dashboard, carpet and seating area. A large portion of it was used to soak the decaying body of Alexander's daughter, Orlenda.

Allowing the fuel to soak into fiber and flesh, he unloaded his cycle and rode down to a secluded area and hid it near the ledge. At a dead run, he made his way back to the coach where he completed his plans. Positioning the RV to follow the trail of the runaway semi, he started the engine and engaged the transmission. As the motor home slowly made its way to the cliff line, he tossed in a fuel soaked torch and slammed the door closed. The slow burning diesel ignited and spread throughout the coach much faster than Dave had imagined. To his approval, it was completely ablaze when it dropped several hundred feet over the ledge into the canyon floor. He had laughed with delight knowing his plan was going to be successful. The loud blast below verified the coach exploded upon contact.

He ran back to join his bike in seclusion and sat down near the ledge to monitor his fire.

Now, he lays the binoculars aside, not surprised that no vehicle has driven by in the ten to fifteen minutes it took him to carry out his deeds. The fiery bus can be seen clearly below the rocky cliff from his location. He notices the fiery flames are lighting up the sky above the pull over. It is burning with such intensity that it has ignited several pines around it. Soon, if not extinguished, it will rage throughout the dry summer forest areas of the mountain. If so, he could care less.

Dave raises his glasses and whispers into the frigid mountain air, "I wish I could have kept you alive until this moment. It would have been a thrill to my soul if I could have seen your eyes as you dropped down the gorge on fire and…alive."

His thoughts venture to other eyes he watched as death over took them. Thoughts filed in his mind were categorized in chronological order. That filing system now allows the most memorable ones to replay across the silvery screen of his memory. A vision comes from a hike across the Himalayans with a fellow soldier while on leave.

He had known her for only a few days before they decided to climb into those high mountains; thus, there was little he could tell authorities about her other than she had slipped over a ledge and fell 500 feet to her death.

The next scene unfolds with the young woman who wanted to teach him to bungee jump. Only weeks after her high school graduation, she drove him to a tall bridge, over 700 feet, to plunge downward toward the rocky shoals below. What a memory that was!

On her bounce upward from the fall, she waved and shouted a greeting of encouragement to him. But her eyes flooded with horror when she saw him undoing the safety latch holding her to the steel railing of the bridge. Her shouts of thrill turned into pleading cries for mercy before she plummeted downward into the rocks, head first. That had been easily explained to the police and her parents since they had been forbidden from leaping off the bridge and since the latching pin, he replaced for hers, showed signs of wear.

He laughs again at the thought of the little redneck girl in Nashville. It was comical to see her crash into the large metal blades of the paddle boat before they churned her into bloody unconsciousness. She was ruled dead from blunt force trauma rather than drowning.

Perhaps, if that little red haired demon had been more patient in the campground, she might have been able to climb the cliff walls with him at the Mesa Verde Cliff Dwellings.

"Wow," he says, "It's always easy if you plan it through!"

Dave pushes backward against the large boulder as if he is in a theater ready to watch a new release. He pulls his feet towards his buttocks, which allows him to rest his elbows comfortably across his knees. From that pose, he is able to focus on the burning RV. The fire of destruction blazes and will soon char the contents of the motor home beyond recognition. Overwhelmed with the rush of adrenalin and the memories of his gory deeds, he fails to observe another motor home has arrived at the scenic overlook. Nor, does he witness the driver exit his coach and walk to the ledge to survey the wreckage below.

The steady strain on his eyes from the magnification of the lens persuades him to drop the binoculars; they sag to his chest and dangle by a cord swung around his neck. Rubbing his eyes to liberate them from blurring, he notices the headlights and outline of the other motor home.

His eyes gain no reprieve as he snatches the glasses from his chest to peer intently at the new arrival. There is no one inside the vehicle, nor can he locate anyone near it. Instinctively, he knows he must locate the driver for he recognizes the coach as the one belonging to his neighbor two nights ago in Oklahoma City. With the glasses pressed tightly to his eyes, he scans the area from the coach downward to the cliff line. All the years of training, along with the blood soaked bodies he has seen, do not prepare him for what he is about to discover. His vision of a moonlit landscape is suddenly invaded with the face of a man standing on the ledge. He zooms in with haste to get a better look and in so doing, he finds himself glaring into the blood red eyes of his latest lover's brother. Flabbergasted, he slams his head backward into the boulder with shock.

The vision, or maybe it was the sharp crash with the boulder, brings him into complete acknowledgement as he speaks aloud.

"He saw me! He knows where I am. I wonder how long he's been there."

He regains his composure, breathes out slowly while returning his binoculars to his eyes. Unlike the Banah, he must have them to observe his nemesis.

Len's twin remains motionless. He glares downward through the canyon into Dave's eyes while opening his mouth like a large lion posed to pounce upon his prey. He growls a threat, unheard by Dave, and menacingly displays his teeth. Large canines shine like ivory needles. The sight of which sends shivers along the spine of the human he hates intensely. Rosti is pleased that his image has shocked the soul of this human. It was his intent and he smiles that his purpose has been achieved.

Dave glares back and for a second, he is reminded of the beautiful red-haired owner of the burning coach. There can be no doubt that the two of them were rooted from the same gene pool; a pool that could only belong to some gruesome monster that was not human.

He returns a soft challenge of his own before shouting into the night air, "Bring it on you..."

The profane dare is heard clearly by the dark figure on the cliff, yet the mad cursing has no effect on him. Dave does not know the one standing before him is Rostislav Gionni, Banah son of Alexander the Nephilim.

Chapter 36

Defiant Folly

" As a bird that wandereth from her nest, so is a
man that wandereth from his place."
Proverbs 27:8

Darkness of night and heavy binoculars pressing tightly against his eye sockets will not hide his blue eyes from the red haired stranger standing a half mile above him. A stranger who needs no flimsy tools of magnification for the blood of a Nephilim leader flows through his veins. Tonight, he promises the stars above with a chilling cry, he will avenge the death of his sister.

"Tonight," he shouts, "I will taste human blood for the first time. I'll drain this murdering man's blood completely from his fragile body and spread his guts into the desert sands. Yes, tonight he will pay for all the innocent blood he has shed. He will pay for the precious lives he has taken from the daughters of the Nephilim; especially, that of my sister."

For a second, he dreads the wrath of his father, for he gave him explicit orders to see that Dave arrived in Copper Town alive. But, he feels the orders were given only because the Nephilim leader was convinced he was not able to destroy this human. He is much stronger than his sister and twice the warrior she could ever hope to be. Tonight he will defy his father, but his victory will demonstrate to the Nephilim leader that he is capable of taking care of any human resistance. Yes, he will defy him, but in the end his value will be discovered in the eyes of his father. Even in that which his older brother Luther had failed, he would be victorious. With a blood chilling growl, Rosti leaps from the ledge in a descent that will take him down into the depths of the canyon.

Chapter 37

A Night's Cry to Battle

"Ointment and perfume rejoice the heart: so doth the sweetness of a man's friend by hearty council."
Proverbs 27:9

Dave curses again as the silhouette vanishes over the ledge like a whisper of smoke. He searches the edge of the cliff with his binoculars to no avail. Rapidly, he moves the glasses upward to the coach and back to the ledge. Curses continue to flow from his lips for there is no sign of the stranger. Twisting on the center knob, he zooms out to widen his field of view which allows him to scan the area below the rocky ledge. Short left-to-right movements aid his gaze into the depths of the canyon which runs in a direct path from the stranger to him.

"My God," he whispers. "He's covered half the distance between us!"

Dave watches the Banah drop with ease from a tall rocky ledge continuing toward him. He leaps over ten foot boulders as if they were high hurdles in a track meet.

He roughly discards the glasses to one side for he knows they will be of no further assistance. The only illumination available now will be supplied by the silvery moon shining directly above. A couple of times he slips in the loose terrain, common to this mountainous region, trying to get to his cycle. His breathing is heavy and his heart pounds recklessly in his chest like a drum. He realizes there may not be sufficient time to retrieve the sword.

There is a slight look of accomplishment on his face as he bends to withdraw the samurai sword from its scabbard. Any intention of celebrating his undertaking is wiped away violently when the stranger's forearm slams along the narrow of his back, lifting him high above the ground. It is a blow that would have taken the life of most men for it was intensified by the speed of the Banah. It sends Dave sailing head-over-heels through the air before his body comes to rest in the top of a scrubby cedar tree.

Rosti hesitates a second trying to decide if he will retrieve the other sword or finish this man off with his bare hands. He decides the latter. He squats with arms outstretched, like a fiendish alien, and roars a villainous war call. The sound echoes throughout the canyon awakening birds on their roost and sends them scattering throughout the darkness of the night in search of safer limbs of refuge. He glares into the tree and swears a personal oath that this man's death will be slow and painful.

Like his sister, Orlenda, he has made the mistake of not knowing that he is battling no ordinary man. While absorbing a blow that would have knocked an elephant from its feet, Dave still maintains a tight grip on his sword. Stretching in the upper most branches of the tree, he wiggles free and drops. His fall is viewed by the Banah as one that will leave him sprawled upon the ground, but Dave lands gingerly on his feet. Slowly, he lifts the sword above his head, bends his knees to lower his body and with his head, he beckons his challenger to come.

Rosti accepts. He rushes in with blinding speed ducking low to his left. The move allows his head to remain atop his shoulders. His red curly hair swirls from the wind of the blade. Little time expires before he leaps high into the air to avoid the second strike. Dave is not startled that his blade did not strike the target of his first blow, although it could have. His intent was to make contact on the second blow. After missing on the first, Dave spins in a complete circle; however, on the second pass his blade is much lower. He correctly guessed that the Banah's next evasive move would be to duck.

Yet, neither is Rosti a stranger to combat. His evasive move sends him over the head of Dave. On his pass, he delivers a violent kick which lands solidly on the right side of the human's head. Dave falls backward shaking his head while a groan escapes from his throat. The slapping action of the kick struck his ear and the force of the compressed air shattered his eardrum. Now, an invisible drum beats loudly in his head and the excruciating pain distracts him for a second. It is a second of elapsed concentration that increases the odds of victory for the son of Alexander. Rosti jumps forward into the air leading with his left foot. In a gyrating move that is near impossible, he spins counter clockwise like a ballet dancer. But this is no dance. His body twists parallel to the ground as if tossed about by a tornado. The Banah's right foot emerges from somewhere among the spinning cyclone and with a quick snapping kick, he strikes Dave's right wrist. The impact from his foot dislodges the sword from the human's hand and sends it sailings through the air before landing several feet beyond the motorcycle.

Rosti lands softly on his toes. There is no hesitation as he instantly charges Dave. His intent is to grab the human in a bear hug and viciously slam him to the ground. A growing hatred for this man overcomes his caution and as a result, his assessment of this human's ability is underestimated. Dave's side step is not anticipated; nor is the reflexive movement which transitions a defensive strategy into a deadly offensive one.

Dave drops to the ground performing a complimentary whirl of his own. A rotation he employs with hopes of sweeping the support leg of the Banah. An action that would cause him to tumble to the ground fails; nevertheless, he is triumphant in grasping a thick branch lying on the ground while rolling to his feet. Securing it with both hands, he swings it hard in the direction of the Banah. The limb comes to a jarring halt before splintering to shreds against the back of Rosti's head.

Dave's accomplishment sends Rosti toppling forward in a woozy stagger. He crashes face first into the same boulder Dave used as a back rest as blood oozes from the back of his head and, unseen by the human, from his bruised and broken nose.

Sliding to the ground, Rosti turns over and slowly sits up, regaining eye contact with the human. Cob webs of confusion which have clouded his mind for days fade; leaving him with clear and rational thoughts. For the first time, he understands why his father did not want him to engage this man in mortal combat. Rosti also knows there will be no leniency for him tonight. He remembers several fights with humans and other Banah, but none of them had inflicted such powerful and painful blows. For a brief moment in time, he imagines that only a Nephilim could strike with such viciousness and power. Nevertheless, he is the son of a Nephilim and if he is to die, he will die fighting.

The stare into Dave's eyes is diverted to the dislodged sword lying close to the motorcycle. He charges forth to retrieve it. But, to his surprise, the human beats him to it. Dave lifts the blade with his right hand, never stopping until he leaps across the seat of his bike. He readies himself in a stance designed many years ago by ancient Samurai warriors. His is not a defensive stand, it is one used to deliver the final thrust of death.

Rosti decides to retrieve the other sword and races to Dave's bike. Surging forth on legs that are still unstable, he removes the sword by its wooden handle. In an attempt to break the human's concentration, he hops upon the seat of the motorcycle. A stance perceived by Dave as somewhat humorous and ridiculous for it causes his bike to wobble. When the wobble becomes calm by the balancing act of the Banah, he threatens Dave with a variety of motions he performs with the magnificent weapon.

Rosti's sword is crafted with a wooden shaft resembling a short javelin. At its tip is a tightly secured razor sharp double-edged blade over twelve inches long. At first appearance, it could be mistaken for a broken spear, but Rosti and Dave both know it is the sword designed and used by Shaka Zulu. And both know how to use it.

Dave sees the crimson rivers flowing heavily from both nostrils of the Banah. Downward they stream into his mouth, spilling over his lower lip before splattering onto his shirt. The sight of Banah blood erases the anxiety previously invading the soul of Rosie's son. Again, curses flow from the mouth of the preacher's son as he prepares to make his final move. Emptying himself with one last damning oath, Dave discharges a blood-curdling yell as he rushes toward Rosti. Alexander's son sees the same approach used previously and laughs for he will be able to easily avoid the arching slice of the ancient blade. He knows Dave's desire is to remove his head and he counters accordingly.

The cycle wobbles again as Rosti's feet drop to the ground. At the same time, his buttocks smack to a rest on the low swung seat of Dave's bike as the Banah thrusts upward with the Zulu. *Maybe*, he thinks, *I will emerge the champion tonight* for he feels the blade of the Zulu sword sink deep into something soft. He seeks to identify the object he penetrated, but is unable to confirm it for his vision is darkened by the reality of his failure to evade the blade of his enemy.

He would never know if Dave sought to sever his body at the waist and he ducked into it, or if Dave had anticipated the low elusive maneuver. Nevertheless, he sees the human's blade. Only moments ago it reflected silvery images of the moon. Now, those reflections are replaced with sickening splotches of scarlet from the deep slash he feels across his throat. His last visions are of Dave's sword coming downward again like an ax in the hand of a lumber jack. The ancient weapon does not halt until it rests beneath the chin of the Banah.

Chapter 38

Origin of the Ten Swords

" Thine own friend, and thy father's friend,
forsake not; neither go into thy brother's house in
the day of thy calamity: for better is a neighbour
that is near than a brother far off."
Proverbs 27:10

"Oh, so it is the swords you want to hear about!" Kara declares, taking a deep breath like a Chemistry professor ready for her lecture.

"First, I must give you some history of the Nephilim. In the beginning there were many Nephilim scattered throughout the world for they were created in prehistoric days. They were sung into existence by the Ancient One long before he created man. Lead by a spiritual creation known as Prince Qadar, a great rebellion took place among them. Some became followers of the Prince while some remained faithful to their maker. The rebellion waxed hot in hopes of overthrowing the Old One and establishing Qadar as the new ruler. However, original plans were snuffed and Qadar was defeated; but it is told that all the faithful Nephilim had been slain through decapitation by the rebels. Soon, the very earth was chaotic and became lost with a vast covering of vapor that endured for centuries."

"So you are saying that my account of Genesis is long after this original creation was destroyed?" asked Rosie.

Kara seems aggravated, but Rosie cannot discern if it is from ignorance of the story or from being interrupted with a question. Kara's facial features are transformed into a grin confirming that it is neither. She continues with the lecture.

"Yes. I guess that's what I'm saying. When the Ancient One re-established order on the Earth, and created man, he divided the remaining seventy Nephilim into ten clans of seven members. He designated areas upon the Earth that they had to dwell within; forbidding them from interfering with the humans he had chosen. People we know as Maseth. All other humans were given to the reign of each clan within their perspective region. They were also given dominion over Maseth who failed to keep the way of the Ancient One. But, some of the Nephilim openly attacked Maseth who were faithfully keeping the ways of the Ancient One. That ultimately brought about clan destruction."

Kara stops for a second to see if Rosie has questions and continues when she discovers she will not be interrupted at this point.

"The Ancient One forged ten swords, at various times, and hid them within the Earth. One sword for each clan and each sword specifically made for that clan. If a clan broke the rules of

175

their book of orders and laws which were provided by the Ancient One, he would chose a warrior among the Maseth who would be led to the sword. Once it was in his hands, he was given power through the sword to destroy that clan. These warriors are known as Bachar. There is no hope of defeating a Bachar warrior once he obtains his sword. Seven of the original clans have been destroyed by Bachar; understandably, only three remain. If the ten swords are brought together, they will become one. This one sword will generate power in the hands of any creation that possesses it. That's why the Nephilim have been searching for the swords for hundreds of years. It's their only hope to defeat the Ancient of Days. With modern technological advancement, specifically the satellite imagery I just showed you, they have been able to locate all ten. Soon, they will bring them together to form the one. When that is accomplished, the Nephilim will gain control of the Earth and all mankind will become their slaves."

Rosie, caring little that she is again going to interrupt, fires a question. "If they have all ten, why have they not been merged?"

"Is it not ironic Rosie that your son is on his way here to deliver the last two? Then, they will be merged into one and it will be Dad's. With it, he will become the new world leader at which time the Nephilim will be fully revealed to all humanity. Never to be masked again by the rules of their Kimriyr."

"So, are you telling me that the swords on the wall have been used to destroy Nephilim clans yet they still have some mystical power?" Rosie inquires.

176

"Yes, to some degree they do…in the hands of a chosen Maseth or perhaps when wielded by another Bachar. But they will never emerge again with full power unless they are forged into one with the others. Needless to say, a sword assigned to an existing clan can yield some degree of energy in the hands of any Maseth. The level of radiance generated depends on the level of commitment to the Ancient of Days that the possessor has at the time he wields it in battle. Your husband was thought to be Bachar, but he was unable to channel the full energy of the sword. A true warrior needs no coaching or training. He and the sword become one upon first contact and are sanctified through the calling and purpose established by the Ancient One. With such a predetermined course, the Bachar always prevails in combat."

Kara notices the mocking roll of Rosie's eyes but is not silenced, determined to complete her story.

"If the Nephilim clans want to exist alongside mankind, they must obey their ordinances. If all become rebellious, then all will be destroyed. It is foretold that the last Nephilim clan cannot be defeated unless the Maseth merge all ten swords into one. Then, one rightful Bachar will come forth with that powerful sword to destroy the last existing clan. Afterwards, the Earth will be repopulated with Maseth only. It is then and only then, that the Ancient One will come to Earth to rule, establish a new world kingdom and to dwell among the Maseth. The Nephilim are determined not to allow this to happen by possessing all the swords."

"I don't know if all that's true or not," quips Rosie. "Sounds pretty far out to me, but tell me more about the individual swords and the clans that were destroyed. If what you are telling me is true, there has to be some historical evidence existing today to confirm it."

"Aha...you are now seeing the light. Let me explain each one to you. We will begin with the first one to the left of the arch."

Chapter 39
The First Egyptian

"My son, be wise, and make my heart glad, that I
may answer him that reproacheth me."
Proverbs 27:11

Alexander's daughter walks to the tall wall containing the swords.
She removes the lowest one to Rosie's left. All are arranged in a
semi-circle with five on the left half of the arch. To the right is
symmetrical spacing for the last five, but only three are displayed.
Assigned sections have been reserved in hopes that John David
will soon deliver the last two to complete the rainbow of swords.

Kara holds the first sword high above her head in a ready
position as if to attack the woman before her. As she lowers it to a
non-threatening position, she begins to speak with knowledge. Her
voice gives no hint of hesitation and rings with a tone of joy...and
authority.

"This is the Egyptian sword of Kamose. He and his father,
Seqenenre Tao II, lived 3,500 years ago. At the same time, a
Nephilim clan relocated from Asia into the region taking the
Egyptians into captivity. They were known as the Hyksos.

179

Historically, they were reckless, vicious and broke all rules of the Kimriyr. They consumed human blood which made them creatures of the night; thus, they were unable to transform into human form by day. They slaughtered many of the Egyptians including their leader Seqenenre. If you study your history books, you will find that a Bachar was called forth. He was the son of the slain leader, Kamose. It was he that destroyed the first of the ten Nephilim clans."

"Again, go look at your history books," Kara challenges, "and see if they don't tell you this. They will also tell you that Seqenenre's body was brutally debased and destroyed. Unknown, however, to humans is the fact that he had been sucked dry of every ounce of blood in his body. Now, come Rosie and look at the blade of the sword. Archeologist all agree that the blade was used in battle as evidenced by the groove marks and nicks on the blade."

Rosie accepts the invitation. She walks to Kara where she is permitted to take the ancient weapon for further examination. The scars on the weapon are clearly visible.

"It looks more like an extra long dagger than a sword," surmises Rosie.

"It is a sword," confirms Kara. "And it's a sword of a Bachar!"

Chapter 40

Sword 2 - Goliath

"A prudent man foreseeth the evil, and hideth himself; but the simple pass on, and are punished."
Proverbs 27:12

She is Banah, half human and half Nephilim. She is the daughter of Alexander Gionni, leader of the Nephilim clan Shachar; interpreted Shining Blackness. She was christened Kara and is the one who replaces the sword of Kamose and retrieves one much larger known as the sword of Goliath. There is no hesitation or feelings of fear as she hands the large sword to Rosie.

John Calvin's widow grasps it with both hands while flexing her legs to support the weight of the large sword. She has no uncertainty that this weapon is a sword. The tip nearly drops to the floor before she gains control of it. Raising it over her head, she poses in a stance which mocks that of Kara's with the Egyptian Kamose. As unexplainable surges of energy course through her body, she experiences feelings of euphoria mixed with an electrifying flow of adrenalin.

Wow, she thinks, *I thought it would be heavier!* Her thoughts are interrupted by the voice of Kara beginning her description of the sword, Goliath.

"That sword is identical in construction to those of the Canaanites, except twice the size. It was used by a Nephilim hybrid conceived while his father was in original form nearly 3000 years ago. Biblically, you know him as Goliath. Yes, Rosie, the Nephilim were there during the battle. The sword was found by the clan and put into the hands of one of their offspring in hopes it would bring defeat to the Maseth. As you know, it did not. They underestimated the great matrix system of the Ancient One. What a paradox, they delivered the sword into the hands of its Bachar. Just a young boy whose name was David. You understand too, that he used it as an adult to bring devastation upon the Canaanites. What you do not know is that in so doing, an entire Nephilim clan was slain through that campaign."

Rosie tosses the sword from one hand to the other amazed at how light it felt. Only moments ago, it seemed as heavy as lead. With each toss, she finds it more easily balanced and with each grasp she experiences surges of energy as if some form, or force, was infiltrating every fiber of her being.

The bronze blade was polished by the giant hands of Alexander the Nephilim. It shimmers with sparkling flashes of red and orange reflections created from the lighting overhead. A large double-edged blade, symmetrical in perfection, greets the hilt before diminishing into a smaller handle section. Although it is a one handed hilt, it was designed for a larger hand. Thus, Rosie easily grasps it with both hands…with room to spare. She moves the blade slowly with figure eight patterns several feet from her body to prevent the tip from striking the floor. A soft whisper of admiration is detected from Kara as she continues to slice the air to shreds with the sword. Alexander's daughter clears her throat loudly preparing Rosie for the explanations to follow concerning the ancestry of her father.

"Breeding with women while the Nephilim is in original form is forbidden. If it happens, the baby is destroyed. That insures the secrecy of Nephilim existence among humans and protects the clans from exposure. Besides, most women die in delivery of such monstrously giant hybrids."

Stepping forward at the precise moment to intercept Rosie gyrating blade, Kara stops the maneuvers. She grasps Rosie's hands in hers and feels their softness. The widowed wife of John Calvin relinquishes the sword to the Banah for she longs to learn of the other swords. She nods with approval while turning to inspect the next sword displayed on the wall behind the Clan Leader's desk.

Chapter 41

Seven Branches for a Third

"Take his garment that is surety for a stranger,
and take a pledge of him for a strange woman."
Proverbs 27:13

Goliath's sword is replaced on the wall which allows Kara to retrieve the next one. Nestled high within the decorative display, this one requires her to stretch fully upon tip-toes before her fingers are able to grasp its hilt. She topples slightly from her efforts. Rosie finds her actions amusing as she resembles a comic book character.

Eventually, the Banah's efforts are rewarded as she frees the latches and drops delicately to the floor with the weapon. As she turns to allow the Preacher's wife a closer observation, she watches Rosie's amusement fade to awe. Everyone displays the same look of terror and trepidation upon first inspection of this bizarre forged sword of seven blades.

Kara steps backward with her right foot and points the sword at her human companion. From that dreadful stance, horror strikes Rosie, for all seven points are clearly defined and each seems eager to pierce her body. In all her travels, Rosie has never seen anything like it. She estimates the total length to be nearly 30 inches. The central blade swells 25 inches from Kara's hand rushing toward the preacher's widow. Three blades issue forth from the top and from the bottom of the main shaft in elbow-type configurations. All seven tips join in unison to collectively send a threatening message to anyone standing before them. Kara tosses the sword and catches it with both hands in a position parallel to the floor. After rotating it to where the ancient inscription is visible, she reads it to Rosie.

"At noon on the sixteenth day of the eleventh month, fourth year of Taiwa era, the sword was made of 100 times hardened steel. Using the sword repels 100 enemy soldiers. Appropriate for the polite duke king."

"This sword," she continues, "was forged in southwest Korea during the Baekje Dynasty in the 4th century. It was a very powerful Dynasty that controlled a large portion of China and western Korea. Again, a Nephilim clan inhabited the area. Their desire for human blood led to a slaughter of thousands of humans before the Bachar was sent forth with this sword. History knows him as King Geunchogo of Baekje, but little else is known. Nephilim history provides an accurate description of Geunchogo. After receiving the sword from the Ancient of Days, he destroyed the clan. Taking no time to rest or gloat about his achievements, he presented this weapon, as tribute, to Eastern Jin as a sign of his praise and respect. Prior to his presentation, he added another inscription to honor Jin."

Alexander's daughter flips the sword over in her hands and reads the second inscription aloud, *"enfeoffed lord."*

She looks at Rosie, pausing for a second before continuing.

"That interpreted means that the King of Wa was subservient to the Baekje ruler. It served to tie the two East Asian countries together as allies. Many think the sword is still housed in the Isonokami Shrine in Nara Prefecture of Japan, but it is not. They have a replica that would be hard for most men to identify as fake. That's the main reason it has never been publicly displayed. Several large shipments of gold and silver were used years ago by Dad to acquire the sword. As you can see, he is not afraid to display it and does so defiantly."

She does not give Rosie an opportunity to handle this particular sword. She drags a larger than normal chair to the wall and replaces it much easier than she removed it. The chair also serves for an effortless removal of the fourth sword resting within the arms of highly polished gold plated hooks.

Chapter 42

Joyeuse the Fourth

"He that blesseth his friend with a loud voice,
rising early in the morning, it shall be counted a
curse to him."
Proverbs 27:14

She continues her monologue with excitement emanating from her voice. Standing in the large chair high above her audience, she bounces the sword in open palms. Her face beams with delight for she is explaining the history of one of her favorite swords.

"This sword was used by Bachar Charlemagne around 800 A.D. He was born in 742 and is still known as one of the greatest rulers in history becoming King of the Franks in 768. After slaying the Nephilim clan that dwelt in Western and Central Europe, he was crowned Emperor of the Romans, a position that he maintained until his death. In the Holy Roman Empire, he was called Charles I, the Empire's first Emperor. During that time, He expanded the Frankish kingdom into areas once controlled by the clan he slaughtered. Human history regards him as the Father of the French and German monarchies. To this day, he is called the Father of Europe."

Rosie's love of history confirms the humanistic portion of the account as factual. She makes no comment concerning Nephilim interaction deciding instead to listen intently. Beside that, she was slowly beginning to trust that Kara was telling the truth. The time has not come for her to understand her part in the destiny of mankind.

Neither will Kara reveal to Rosie that she is one of few humans to gain the Nephilim knowledge of the swords…and live! She lightly tosses the sword to the human.

"The sword you are holding, Rosie, is called Joyeuse. There are two swords today that are displayed claiming to be Joyeuse. One is kept in the Weltliche Schatzkammer in Vienna and the other is at the Louvre in France. Neither of them belonged to Charlemagne. The one you hold was his personal sword forged by the Ancient One. It has been responsible for removing the heads of seven Nephilim. Subsequently, he used it to behead the Saracen Commander, Corsuble, who was in league with the Nephilim. Later, he employed it to knight his friend Ogier the Dane. After his death, the sword was held by Saint Denis Basilica. And before it was taken to the Louvre, it was carried at the coronation of all French kings."

Rosie's small hands tightly squeeze the long golden hilt. Impressions materializing on her palms and fingers are caused by diamonds, too numerous to count, embedded decoratively in the grip. She looks closely at the hilt and discovers the crowned pommel consists of two halves forged as one with gold.

"Dad's acquisition of this sword was by force. Monetary offers in exchange for the sword were refused by the Louvre. That was unfortunate for them. It was one of the few times that Dad took human lives by dining on their blood. According to other members of Shachar, it was a brutal massacre. He replaced the sword with a replica…and do you know something funny?"

Rosie shakes her head that she does not.

"All attempts to authenticate their sword have failed. Imagine that, will you? Rosie, you hold Joyeuse, the real one!"

A surge of energy that could only be attributed to the life force of the sword erupts within Rosie's body. She is aware of her heavy breathing and knows her heart throbs rapidly. She is reluctant to surrender this particular sword to Alexander's daughter who is reaching for it with extended arms.

Somewhere in the confines of time, she agrees to relinquish it to the Banah. For a second, the act leaves her frustrated and in agony. She feels as if a protective fence separating her from a pack of hungry hyenas has been demolished.

Kara replaces the sword from her chair and removes the fifth one. Turning quickly, and with no warning, she tosses it to Rosie and watches her snatch it from the air.

Chapter 43

Mercy for Five

"A continual dropping in a very rainy day and a
contentious woman are alike."
Proverbs 27:15

"You are holding the sword of King Edward the Confessor. Some think it was broken in battle, but it was not. It was actually forged, as you see it, by the Ancient One. Maybe its design illustrates his sense of humor, or maybe it was so formed to confuse the Nephilim clan it destroyed. No one knows for sure, but the blade was not broken in battle."

Kara watches Rosie's eyebrows rise in confusion, or perhaps disbelief. She knows there are many things she must explain to this woman and little time to do it. There is an urgency to continue, for her time is running out to initiate the plan.

"Yes Rosie, Edward was chosen as a Bachar. His sword is known as the Sword of Mercy, but I can assure you there was no mercy given to the Nephilim clan he destroyed in the year of 1066. It was his final victory, for history would know him as the last Anglo-Saxon king of England. As you may know, England was conquered by the Normans. What you do not know is that Dad and

Clan Shachar planned and equipped the Conquest. In return for his assurance of victory for the Normans, Dad demanded only the broken sword of Edward."

Rosie ponders while twirling the famed Sword of Mercy and murmurs, "How did I learn to handle a sword in this manner? I've seen it done in movies, but those performances were by professionals who spent years mastering it."

She twirls it repeatedly under the examining eyes of Kara. Faster and faster it goes until it appears as a blur. Light begins to surge brilliantly from the whirling motions, plastering the walls with an iridescent and beautiful show of light. Within seconds, they change into a multitude of interlacing rainbows then separate and merge into a multicolored sphere. The sphere expands around Rosie until it completely swallows her within its dome. Unbeknownst to her, it serves as an impenetrable force field of protection. The power she felt from the Joyeuse is incomparable to that she experiences from this magnificent weapon grasped tightly within her small hand.

Kara continues gazing at the spectacle before her, gaping at the display in awe and disbelief. She never imagined that a mere human female would be able to handle this mystical sword with such ease. A look of unimaginable revelation sweeps her facial features. She has witnessed something no one knows, or has suspected, and vows it will remain her secret. Kara extends her arms for the sword. She is consumed with fear that Rosie might refuse to surrender the weapon; yet time is slipping away and she must continue the history of the blades.

To defeat Alexander, Rosie realizes she must acquire more knowledge of the swords. That information cannot be gained until she forfeits the sword she has. Yet, she discovers it is no easy task to concede her possession. But, pure determination enables her to drop it into the open hands of the Banah. The power she experienced drains from her soul along with the vanishing orb of brilliant lights. With a downcast face, she listens to the summary of The Sword of Mercy.

"Oliver Cromwell is known for ordering the melting down of ancient artifacts for scrap gold and metal. In so doing, he was actually hoping to find and destroy the authentic sword of Edward. Oliver feared the sword might surface again and threaten his reign. He understood better than any other that the Sword of Mercy used for bestowing knighthood was not authentic. To this day there are few, if any, which believe the Sword of Mercy used by the British, is anything but a counterfeit. The Nephilim know it is. What you see in my hand is the authentic Sword of Mercy that the Norman leader, William, presented to my Dad."

Chapter 44

Wallace's Weapon

"Whosoever hideth her hideth the wind, and the
ointment of his right hand, which bewrayeth
itself."
Proverbs 27:16

With the same degree of effortlessness, Kara drags the large chair
to the right side of the display and leaps into it to remove the upper
most sword. It is the sixth that Rosie will exam. Carefully she lifts
it, still in a scabbard, and vaults to the floor. Leisurely, she eases
the blade from its protective case before offering it to the widow –
blade first!

Rosie slaps upward with both hands to sandwich the
beautiful sword in a grasp midway along the fuller. The Preacher's
widow is not hesitant to inspect the razor sharp edges. Both
emerge from the guard, or *chappe*, along the forte. The
dangerously honed edges finally meet at the point where they join
with the central ridge. Overall, the length of the shaft is 4 feet and
4 inches. It weighs over 6 pounds, but Rosie tosses it into the air
with ease and as gravity begins to tug it downward to the floor, she
grabs it by the grip with both hands, pommel down. Jumping

upright she assumes an ancient ready pose she should not know. With a quick glance over her left shoulder, she pivots to face Kara. The massive blade points to the ceiling while the edges give an impression of indecisiveness as to which will consummate a merger with the neck of the Banah. The fear that struck Kara moments ago has vanished; she merely laughs at Rosie. She shows no signs of flinching, nor does her voice quiver as she begins to describe the weapon to John Calvin's widow.

"My friend, you are holding the sword of William Wallace, a Scottish knight who lived from 1272-1305. He was the great champion of the Scottish people during the wars in which they acquired their independence from England. Unknown to your kind, part of a Nephilim Clan was slain by William at the Battle of Stirling Bridge in 1297 with that sword. Centuries before, the clan relocated into that area by empowering Viking raiders who captured and populated it along with them. Once established, they began to consume human blood."

"Rosie, it's about time you noticed that throughout the history of man if a society was secretive, or isolated, it was usually ruled by a clan of Nephilim. Seclusion enables them to keep their thirst for blood, and practices associated with it, secretive."

Rosie listens. She maintains her pose with William's sword like a medieval statue chiseled from solid rock. Not a word does she utter; she elects to listen to the Banah relate the story of the sword and the creature that collected it.

"Later in 1298, William destroyed the remainder of that Nephilim Clan at the Battle of Falkirk. Subsequently, Dad took the sword from him prior to his execution for treason by King Edward I of England in 1305. It was replaced by another one very similar to the real one you are holding. The replica is displayed at the National Monument in Stirling, Scotland. I think it's comical, in a way, that Scottish authorities concede to this day that they do not believe the sword is authentic. How does it feel, my friend, to hold the most famous sword in the world?"

Twice now, the words *my friend* has echoed within the study. The words which led to Rosie's discomfort now heighten her anxiety with confusion. Although meant to be menacing, they convey to her an underlying hint, or desire, for companionship.

After leaping back into the chair, Kara turns patiently reaching for the sword of fame. For the first time since assuming her statue-like stance, Rosie bounds forward with the sword to thrust upward with a spearing action toward Kara. Alexander's daughter still shows no evidence of fear. She does not move, nor does she blink an eye. The Banah slaps the blade with both hands as Rosie had previously. When she feels the human's release of the sword, she flips it spinning end-over-end into the air. It is a spinning action that duplicates, or mocks, the one Rosie used earlier. After a near collision with the ceiling, the sword spirals downward and before it can crash to the floor, Kara quickly snatches it by the handle with her left hand. She slips it into the old scabbard and reverently returns it to its rightful place on the wall.

Chapter 45

The Seventh Sword, a Bonaparte

"Iron sharpeneth iron; so a man sharpeneth the
countenance of his friend."
Proverbs 27:17

Ten swords for ten clans of Nephilim; each sword formed by the
Ancient of Days. In the end, the swords are destined to be one.
Whosoever forges the ten into one will acquire unequaled power
from the Creator of the swords. Thus, the race accelerates between
man and Nephilim to collect the ten. It is a race which humans are
unaware; however, Nephilim are not ignorant of the final merging
of the swords. The display upon the wall of Alexander's study
attests to Nephilim awareness and serves as evidence of their
progress in claiming all ten. Ownership of the ten shall
unquestionably make Alexander the leader of the remaining clans.
Ultimately, it will establish him with dominion over humanity;
Maseth and non-Maseth alike. He has eight of the ten collected on
the wall of his study and, expediently, is monitoring the delivery of
the last two to Copper Town.

The dark walnut walls of his two-story study are
impressively decorated with large monitors, televisions and

computers. Some of his technological advancements have not been revealed to man. The greatest of his accomplishments, however, is the display of the Swords of Bachar adorning the wall behind his desk. Ten spot lights individually cast their brilliance upon the sword they have been set to highlight, including the vacant locations of the two missing ones. Pommels of each sword are positioned inwardly along the graceful archway of his exhibit with blades pointing outward. Together, they look like rays of light, sparkling from highly polished blades not formed by man or Nephilim. Outward from a large and empty rectangular center, they flow like golden rays of sunshine.

Each sword is held by golden hooks. With a close inspection, it can be readily discerned that something very special is to be placed in the vacant center section. Its magnificent design seems to be waiting to possess the object for which it has been constructed.

The case is covered with soft leather dyed purple. Standing nearly eight feet tall, its top extends upward beyond the fifth and sixth swords and serves to divide the arch into two congruent halves. With a width of three feet, the purple surface is twenty-four square feet. No seam is to be seen, for there is none. At the top, curved molding made of pure silver and gold come together in the center creating a large almond. Spouting forth from the almond are ten smaller chaplets, each with flowers streaming forth like bouquets of roses. There are ten chaplets for ten swords and one large almond for the sword the ten will become.

Ivory mounted with polished clasps of bronze make up the frame. The smooth surfaced clasps reflect the subdued scarlet lighting shining from a large spot light above Alexander's desk. He spent many nights sitting and glaring with disgust at his incomplete collection. Lately, a Nephilim smile has replaced his empty scowl as his dreams seem near to fulfillment.

Down each side of the frame are five smaller, yet identical, almonds. Five on the left and five on the right - symmetrically placed. In the center of each is a brilliant gem. Each gem has been cut to the same size and contains the same number of facets, yet each is different in color. To the left and starting at the top is a garnet and below the garnet is one of topaz. Below that is a ruby and below it is an emerald. At the bottom, is a sapphire. From top to bottom they are: garnet, topaz, ruby, emerald, and sapphire.

Different gems are fashioned into the right side. At the top is a sparkling diamond, followed by a jacinth, an agate, an amethyst, and one of jasper.

Each stone is crafted as a representation of an individual clan and the geographic region of their original dwellings. Regions selected not by Nephilim choice, but by the Ancient One.

It is from this display that Kara starts to remove the seventh sword which is labeled not with inscription, but with the jacinth stone. From atop her chair, she stretches forth while exercising extreme care and lifts the sword from its golden hooks. She steps gently to the floor with the weapon although it is contained in a scabbard.

Her cautious act appears as if she is holding an infant wrapped in a blanket. Turning with the same degree of care, she faces Rosie and caressingly slides the sword from its casing. This blade shines like none of the others which Rosie examined. The Nephilim's daughter makes no attempt to let the widow handle her favorite sword as she begins her explanation of the nature of the weapon.

"This sword belonged to Napoleon Bonaparte. As you might know, he had a series of victories over every opposition he encountered. Those victories gave France a very dominant position in continental Europe. He came into possession of this sword never knowing its origin. The cruel and inhumane actions of the Nephilim dwelling in Russia stimulated Napoleon to invade the country. Many think that invasion was the turning point of his fame and power. That's quite the contrary! The seventh Nephilim clan was obliterated during his invasion of that country.

When he finished his campaign, his weapon was rendered powerless and so was he. As Bachar, he forgot the ways of the Maseth and fell into the hands of the Nephilim Clan, Ruy. Ruy had supplied and planned the Sixth Coalition. It seems, even with Nephilim, rebellion and destruction often comes from within. Clan Ruy exiled him to the island of Elba from which he escaped. But soon after being recaptured, he died in confinement on the island of Saint Helena."

Flipping her hair over her shoulders, the blue eyed Banah will not be hindered with questions.

"Rosie if you examine historical records closely, you will find that a gold-encrusted sword Napoleon carried was auctioned off in France for more than 6.4 million dollars. The winner of that auction was never identified. But you, my friend, are the first human to know…it was my Dad.

Chapter 46

The Life of a Pilot

"Whoso keepeth the fig tree shall eat the fruit thereof: so he that waiteth on his master shall be honoured."
Proverbs 27:18

Lyrics of a song by Queen ring, *who wants to live forever?* As the song continues blasting loudly from the Golden Oldies radio station, it prompts a response from the driver.

"Long time since I've heard that song," Jim shouts over the roar of the music and the engine of his Hummer. He rarely tuned into any other radio station and today he is rewarded for the song he listens to is his all-time favorite. The music penetrates the depths of his mind and brings to memory the first time he heard it.

Working years for the Nephilim has brought him to the point of often asking himself, "Why would anyone want to live forever when love lies dying."

He only wanted to fill every minute of the day with pleasures of the world. When it came to pleasure, there was very little he had not yet experienced and in the end he felt there would be no stone left to overturn.

Through the open window of his vehicle he sings the lyrics along with Queen to a policeman monitoring his speed from a marked cruiser. Since he is not guilty of speeding, he dares not to provoke the officer with any gestures that might appear disrespectful; besides, the policeman cannot hear the words of a love that lies dying. Beyond the cruiser he yells bravely, "When there's no more pleasure for me…cast my ashes."

On the other side of town, Jim accelerates to 70 mph and sets the cruise control. Although the speed limit is higher in Nevada than most states, he knows from experience the permissive margin of error is less. The Nevada Highway Patrol allows a mile or two above any posted speed limit; however, they do not engage in debate with speeders about the margin of error. Those desiring to debate the difference are often taken to jail after watching their vehicles disappear behind a tow truck.

He is excited and eager to rendezvous with the woman he met at the brothel; wisely, he has determined another speeding ticket to his tally is not in his best interest. Although Alexander thought it nothing to make quick phone calls to get him dismissed from tickets, and sometimes out of more serious problems, Jim did not like asking his employer for such favors. Creative lyrics flow from his lips with a resolve, "I'll just take it easy tonight!"

As the lyrics and the music fade away, his mind rapturously explodes with imaginations. The increasing distance between him and Copper Town would make it hard for the Nephilim to read his thoughts. So, finally he can enjoy the privacy of his cognizance.

Jim's most pleasurable memories stemmed from female companionship. Yes, he was known as a "ladies man" and by definition, he supposes it to be true. It was not a vain prideful confession in which he thought women were drawn to him, but a simple acknowledgement that he preferred their company rather than men. Although his encounters with women involved sex, and a lot of it, he longed for a more meaningful relationship. If only he could find that "right" woman to settle down with, then maybe his life could be complete. One thing was for sure, he did not like being alone. Thus, he would welcome the arms of any of his previous lovers if the opportunity was available. It thrilled him to listen to women as they confided in him of things they loved, pleasures they desired, mistakes they had made along with some of their wildest fantasies.

"Yep," he continues to sing, "I love 'em all!"

He thinks of a day when he might settle down with one, but as of now there is no single woman that could keep his eyes from drifting to another. This little lady he met in the brothel might just be the one. He laughs from the thought and explains to himself why.

"You know, I really like honesty…she sure is candidly truthful. The things she told me were near unbelievable. And you know something Jim? She's had enough experiences with men that she'd never search for greener pasture!"

"Ha!" he laughs. "That's one thing we'd never fight about. When the time's right, I'll share my life of immorality with her."

There is not much Jim dislikes in life beyond liars. He separates himself from such people, refusing to be associated with them unless business deems it a necessity.

Jim's thoughts return completely to his driving as he negotiates the dangerous turn-about in Fernley. Midway through, he veers toward the center curb to avoid a car meandering across the yellow line toward him. He lays down on the horn to warn the driver that his texting while driving is not only illegal, but has caused him a near collision. Normally, he is not easily provoked to anger; today is an exception. A series of repeated honks emerge from the Hummer's horn and are sandwiched with repetitious hand gesture he freely gives to the driver.

"Idiot!" he yells.

Once he is back in the lane and free from the crazy driver he confesses, "Perhaps that was not the best way to handle that situation, but it worked."

He calms and voices his synopsis of the driver one last time, "Idiot!"

The pilot's pulse rate returns to normal as he merges unto I-80 west. He smiles again knowing he is within fifteen minutes of arriving at the Mustang Ranch. Tonight, he will dig deep into his pocket to claim the undivided attention of his new love. Afterwards, she will freely be his for two days, since she does not have to work.

He is somewhat exhausted after the drive and wishes Alexander had allowed him to bring the helicopter. He felt like pushing the issue before leaving Copper Town, but knew that a Nephilim's answer is always final and never debatable. Besides, he liked his employer and did not want to provoke him. It didn't matter to Jim who was running this stupid world. He would always have a place in the Nephilim Empire; regardless if he was called a slave, a servant, or a prince. Nothing ever changes, regardless of who is in charge.

After accelerating to intestate speed, Jim remembers the beautiful woman he met in Mexico a few years ago while running some errands for his employer. Perhaps she was meant to be the one for him for he could not erase her from his memory, even though he tried day and night for years; she was always on his mind.

The trip to Mexico rated among the most enjoyable experiences of his life. He drove the newly purchased Hummer and wore out two sets of tires traveling on the secondary roads. The road surface was composed of dirt and rock, and often the rocks were what he classified as boulders. Rarely was he able to drive above 30 or 45 mph, but the trip was great.

He entered the country at Nogales traveling along the Sierra Madre mountain range until it descended into the more populated areas of Guanajuato. From there he traveled better roads down into the jungle areas of Campeche to pick up cargo for Alexander. Jim expressed his appreciation and gratitude to the Leader of Shachar for allowing his trip to be made by automobile. Alexander countered by granting extra travel time to allow his pilot to take his vacation. Letters in Spanish were provided, and were used a few times when he was stopped by Mexican Police. It was hard for the helicopter pilot to comprehend the vastness of the Nephilim influence throughout the world. He wished he could have read the letters, but desired more that he could have spoken their language. Nevertheless, that barrier did not prevent his trip from being anything but joyous.

From Campeche, Jim decided to return on primary roads. He traveled north spending an exciting night in Mexico City before traveling to Zacatecas. There it was he met the lovely woman who stole his heart.

Gripping the steering wheel until his knuckles turn white, he breathes heavily remembering again that brief and unforgettable encounter.

Jim booked two nights at the Casa Sta Lucino hotel in Zacatecas, one of the oldest hotels in the city. It was remodeled and modernized, yet the owners had maintained the uniqueness of its old design. His suite had ceilings nearly fourteen feet high with an entry room containing a couch and desk with chair. Off to the right of the entry was a bedroom with two queen size beds, a television, microwave, refrigerator, and a small balcony which overlooked the busy street.

He passed through during a long week of festivities. The street was crowded with musicians. People both young and old danced through the slow moving traffic of the one way street. The entire area was heavily posted with police while military vehicles cruised regularly on patrol. He had never felt safer at any time in his life. Standing on the tiny balcony, he saw her for the first time as a touring bus, with seats on the roof, made its way up the street.

A guide stood on the upper level and spoke over the intercom system. He pointed - for assistance to those seated on the upper level - to different structures while communicating in the native tongue points of interest. When the bus slowed to a stop in front of his balcony, he found himself eye-to-eye with those sitting on top. Slowly scanning the eyes of each tourist, he was jolted by surprise at the most delightful woman he had ever laid eyes on. She too, was locked into his gaze. It was a stare he could not escape. Day and night his mind returned to it with a thousand explanations, but was never satisfied with any. The look lasted only for ten seconds or so, but a lifetime of experiences passed between them in that brief span of time.

She never smiled. Her soft brown eyes reflected hurt, pain, and hatred for the Americano. Somewhere deep within her, an emotion erupted unexpectedly; an emotion of love fueled by a desire for the unknown. She desired to know him and his own desire was not masked. Both were flooded with undeniable passion that manifested itself within them like a tidal wave. Their longing, one for another, was short for they were separated when the bus pulled out and made its way down the crowded street. Although Jim watched her until the bus was out of sight, she never looked back. He spent restless hours trying to sleep that night, but sleep would not come. Nor, could he erase her image from his thoughts. It was imprinted into the depths of his mind forever.

Later in the night, Jim stepped onto the balcony to pass the night watching long lines of Mariachi Bands parading down the street. With his elbows bracing him for support, he leaned over for a better view of the spectacular festivities. Permitting his eyes to scan the busy street that night, he nearly fell over the rail when he discovered that once again, he was looking deep into the eyes of the beautiful Latino woman. She stood at the bus stop opposite the hotel. It appeared she was waiting for the next bus.

Her head was forward but her eyes had been cast upward in search of him. She noticed his arrival on the balcony long before he saw her. Once again, their eyes meet with a display of love and understanding of which both had spent a life time searching; yet, neither had found.

She stepped off the curb into the street and began a stroll to his hotel. The embrace of their eyes could not be broken. To this date, Jim never witnessed such kindness, compassion and courage portrayed in the eyes of a woman than hers. They were still the most beautiful pair of eyes he had ever looked into. She watched him intently, waiting for a gesture, or words of encouragement, to remove the thread of fear she bottled within. Although he too feared rejection, a surge of boldness over took him enabling him to motion for her to come to him. With a slow nod of her head, her hair bounced tenderly on her shoulders as she disappeared through the hotel entry below his balcony.

At that moment, Jim's pulse intensified and his breathing became heavy. Sweat ebbed from his pores making his pale skin glisten as if it had been waxed with lotion. He could hardly move as he made his way to the door with intentions of meeting her in the lobby. His plans were flawed for when he opened the door she stood breathing as heavily as he…at his door. A form fitting dress clung to her body with a long, slit from above her knees to her ankles. A roll of intricately carved buttons held the garment together.

The upper buttons were nearly undone to her waist when Jim opened the door. He stood watching as slender fingers (tipped with manicured nails detailed with bright red polish and topped with yellow flowers) continued to unfasten the remaining buttons. Never taking her eyes from his, she opened the dress. Smooth and glistening skin the` color of molasses invited his touch. Jim reached forth, took her hands and tenderly brought her into his room.

She spoke no English, he spoke no Spanish but the passion boiling within them needed no interpretation. The sounds of her moans and the feel of her fingertips as they explored his body were never forgotten. No softer kiss had Jim experienced and her breath was sweeter than wine. Truly, within seconds, he had fallen head-over-hills in love that night. But when the light of day pushed away the drum beats of the bands and darkness of his room, he found himself alone. Sometime in the night, he had surrendered into a peaceful sleep from the pleasure of her sweetness. As he slept, she had dressed and slipped away into the darkness.

Jim searched for her and tried asking the clerk about her. All through the day and late into the next night, he spent hours searching the streets and shops…to no avail. An extension of his stay by another day proved unsuccessful in locating his new love. With despair and a heavy heart, he departed for Copper Town with Alexander's package realizing he would never see her again.

Jim would never know months later the little woman would bear him a daughter. Nor, would he know that the night spent with him had been to escape the brutal attacks of a drunken and jealous husband. A man who never showed appreciation for the beautiful and compassionate woman he married and would likewise never know the love and compassion she had given to a gringo. It was a love that refused to fade from their hearts.

Chapter 47

Conquistador

"As in water face answereth to face, so the heart
of man to man."
Proverbs 27:19

Shimmering with brilliance similar to the moon's reflections upon a pool of water, the silver bands decorating the locket and *chappe* of the scabbard reflect the light of Alexander's study. Two other silver straps, crafted along the black holster, refuse to be subdued by the luster of the terminal bands. The four of them stand brilliantly in contrast against the wood.

Rosie does not recognize the type of wood used to fashion the sword's scabbard. She does note its polished texture compliments the protruding gold handle. The handle's grip is cross-woven with silver thread-like strands which provided a secure grasp for the Conquistador who bore it many years ago. Swelling within her is a desire to own this spectacular weapon. Although forged for destruction and death, the extravagant artistic configuration encourages her; she extends her arms toward Kara with a plea for possession. It is the eighth, and the last, Kara will remove. There was no need for the chair to retrieve this one for it was mounted in the middle of the right arch. Turning to face Rosie, she considers the outstretched arms. Then with slow and deliberate submission, she relinquishes possession of the sheathed sword.

Coldness permeates Rosie's hands as she grips the weapon; a coldness which sends a chill of excitement through her body. She secures it with a death grip. The handle cross guard is gold and formed with a semi-spherical cup common to many one-handed swords used by the sixteenth century Spanish Conquistadors. Silver threads, identical to those on the grip, divide the cup into six triangular scenes. They are not identical for each scene portrays a separate and long forgotten battle.

Midway through the scabbard, Rosie's left hand grips it tightly. With her right hand, she quickly frees the blade from its protective case. The brilliance of the silver support bands fade in the presence of the shining metal of the two-edged sword. Its solid steel blade, forged many years ago in Toledo, has been polished to a spectacular shine by the hands of its Nephilim owner.

"That sword was brought here twenty-one years ago from Mexico by Jim," Kara states.

"He retrieved it for Dad while testing a new off-road vehicle designed by the American Motors Corporation called a Hummer. Actually, they designed it in 1979 as the Humvee - a High Mobility Multipurpose Wheeled Vehicle. It was delivered to the armed forces in 1985. In 1992, the company introduced it as a civilian vehicle called the H1, or Hummer. Since the design originated from the mind of a Banah, Dad used Jim as a test driver over the back roads of Mexico. Jim really enjoyed that trip. Called it his vacation time, but his major assignment was to bring the sword back."

She stops for a second to watch the blade's glow intensifying like a flame in the hands of the widow. With widened eyes, she continues.

"It has really kept the Nephilim wondering about its origin. Beyond a shadow of doubt it is a weapon forged for a Bachar, but there's never been a clan in that region. In fact, only Dad's Clan Shachar has dwelt in the Americas. The sword was discovered on an excavation site near Campeche, Mexico. So, it is authentic and was obviously used by a Spanish Conquistador in the sixteenth century. Many feel it is the sword that belonged to Hernando Cortes. What really matters is the fact that when it was handled by a Maseth employee, it blazed with fire…like it is now. Needless to say, Dad was notified immediately."

Rosie lays the scabbard on the Nephilim leader's desk and moves cautiously around the room with the sword. She resembles a SWAT member looking for assailants while sweeping a dark room. The sword reflects the light from above, but there is an undeniable radiance coming from it that cannot be explained by either the wielder or the Banah observer. She makes large figure eight patterns in the air followed by vertical slashes and punctuated with horizontal stabs. A soft steady buzz resembling the vibration of a cell phone issues throughout the room caused by the ceaseless motions of the sword.

"Actually, for the first time since their creation, the entire Nephilim Empire is in total confusion. The last three Bachar swords have been found in North America."

Rosie understands she is not expected to respond for Kara does not stop with her saga. Nor does the widow of John Calvin McGarney cease to fight the shadows advancing on her from every direction.

"Dad knew the one forged to slay Shachar would be found here, but he did not expect to find the other two on this continent.

The one your husband took with him to Riley was found in Nevada at Area 51. It was forged by Masamune under the guidance of the Old One. I don't know if you recognize that name or not, but Masamune was the greatest metallurgist of all time. In return for his faithfulness to the Ancient of Days, he was permitted to forge similar weapons of his own. That explains how his swords were far superior in beauty and quality than any others ever forged. The one he fashioned for the Bachar was in 1288 A.D. But, it was never used against a clan. It remained in the hands of Masamune's people and was passed down from one Shogun to another.

In 1939 that particular weapon, known as the Honjo Masamune, was given to the Kii branch of the Tokugawa family. They gave it to a police station in Mejiro, Japan in December of 1945. Shortly thereafter, in January of 1946, it was given to Sgt.

Coldy Bimore of the United States. Sgt. Bimore brought it to the states where it was reported lost somewhere in the Nevada desert near a place known as Area 51. All the efforts in and around Area 51 by the government was actually led by Dad in his successful search for the sword.

The tenth one was found recently in the coal mines at Riley. Again, that too baffles the Nephilim. It was the sword of the Bachar from which Shaka Zulu was permitted to use as a pattern for his warriors. Your son should be here tonight with those two and the collection of the ten will be complete."

Rosie's fight with the shadows comes to an end. She has heard every word from the Banah, but now interjects with a question concerning the soft buzz of her new weapon.

"Kind of makes you wonder where the producers of Star Wars got their idea for the sound effects of the light sabers...don't you think ?"

Kara knows the answer. Yet, she is astonished that this human has correctly observed factual natures of the swords. Nevertheless, she lies when she answers, "You've got a wild imagination, Rosie!"

There is no hint of warning as Rosie leaps atop Alexander's desk. The sword swirls with such rapid movements it cannot be seen. Light flowing from the blade sparkles like neon signs in Las Vegas. They grow in intensity like rainbows and form smaller orbs mixed with as many colors. The strange and eerie spheres grow powerfully and spread throughout the large room until they all surround the dancing warrior. As suddenly as they were formed, they collide into one giant sphere and envelope Rosie in a protective and impenetrable force field. Rosie continues with her dance of death by jumping to the top of a file cabinet where she destroys two or three imaginary opponents. The aura of her protective bulb goes as she goes.

Sliding to the floor, she races across the room leaping from one piece of furniture to another. Adversaries only she can see fall one by one as she slays them with the beautiful sword. The displays of light from one series of moves remain sparkling when she moves to generate another.

Kara stands with mouth open. Her eyes beam with astonishing adoration accompanied with fear and surprise. As the room fills with exhibitions of illumination, the Banah finds a love evolving within her for this human. A love she has never experienced. It is the compassion in which one would die for another and causes her half-human soul to yearn for union with that of Rosie's. That desire triggers a vow that she will assist this beautiful woman with her plans to battle her Nephilim father, Alexander Gionni.

"Rosie," she starts. "Come, the afternoon is near gone and darkness approaches bringing with it the full moon. Dad and the whole town are preparing to meet your son. Let's leave that we might warn him. My friend, I will serve you until death do us part."

The widow listens and knows this Banah speaks truth. She too, has discovered that this blond haired woman (which she declared to her husband to be nothing but a floozy) is now her one and only friend in this god desolate place.

"Fine," she says, "until death sees us parted! I swore to take the head of your Father so I hope you are prepared to see it happen. As for this sword, I will not let it go!"

"It's definitely meant for you," Kara answers as she retrieves the Bonaparte for her own use.

"Hurry now, let us be on our way!"

Chapter 48

Visions of Hunger

"Hell and destruction are never full; so the eyes of
man are never satisfied."
Proverbs 27:20

"What a night!" Dave declares to himself.

"Boy, it's been several years since I've experienced anything like it. Good thing this is the loneliest road in the nation"

He spent nearly an hour carrying Rosti's body back to the burning motor home. He was so tired that the body of the Banah barely cleared the ledges beneath the cliff when he tossed it over. Nor, was time wasted as he backed Rosti's coach up the road several hundred feet. That enabled him to get up enough speed to lock the brakes near Len's crash site. Convincing tread marks on the pavement veered off the road and downward toward his sister's flaming RV. Purposefully, he maneuvered the second vehicle to the left of the one already ablaze. On the descent, it barely missed Rosti's body. That would have been hard to explain, but as of now, it should look as if the driver attempted a leap to safety.

Dave declares to the burning scene below him, "The police should see this as an accident. No evidence of anything else!"

He turns and wastes no time retracing the steps to his cycle.

"At this point, I'm so tired, I really don't care!"

Again, he speaks to himself, but is not persuaded of his truthfulness. His laboring betrays him for he quickly repacks the swords and other items removed earlier from the saddle bags. In record time, he is racing the bike down into the valley floor towards Ely. As he enters the city limits, he sees the first car moving eastward on Highway 50 and understands that within an hour, the driver will report the mountain pass accident. That report will send troopers and emergency personnel racing into the mountains in a futile attempt to rescue any survivors.

It is almost dawn and the hunger pangs gnawing in his stomach overpower his need for sleep which is evidenced by the tugging of his eyelids. A ten minute stop at the convenience store is all he requires to top off with gas, wolf down a tall cup of coffee cooled by ice cubes, and swallow a couple packs of sugar frosted donuts. A canned soda along with some of his favorite candy bars are tucked carefully into a saddle bag. To avoid suspicion, he slowly cruises through the little town heading west to Copper Town.

A couple of hours later, rays from the rising sun begin to warm his leather clad shoulders and the top of his back. They promise, and warn, that before noon they will blister any exposed areas of his skin.

Midmorning finds him riding into Eureka. He stops at the only little diner in town where he finally eats a breakfast that has some substance. The gnawing hunger in his gut disappears before the food on his plate. He squanders no time before starting a flirtatious conversation with a waitress twice his age. Promises are made. He will take her for a ride on his bike when he returns in a couple of days, and if she spends the night with him, it will be one she will never forget. She only laughs for Dave reminds her of a son she has not seen in years. Besides, his talk is cheap and reveals nothing she has not heard many times before. A talk she thinks should be added to the daily menu.

After breakfast, filled with food and the frustration of rejection, Dave fills the gas tank again to continue his journey. He makes a promise to stop in on his way back and convince her that she really wants to spend time with him…one way or the other.

For now, he decides to ride a few more miles into the Monitor Mountain range, find a shady isolated area where he can spread his sleeping bag and get a few hours of sleep. If all goes as planned, he will ride into Copper Town at sunset.

Chapter 49

Poetry of a Madman

"As the fining pot for silver, and the furnace for
gold; so is a man to his praise."
Proverbs 27:21

A muffled whisper gently slips through his lips, "I know you are
there, you monstrous vampire. I have always known that you were
there!"

He runs to an old discarded lawn chair and retrieves his
smudged sketch book. Repeatedly, he has repaired the webbing of
his treasured chair with wire from hangers rescued from the town's
trash dumpsters. Decoratively, he has intertwined the wire with
ropes and twine to secure patches of leather and cloth for extra
padding. Every single patch is sized to fit, aided by his large
hunting knife. A knife that now rests, point deep, atop his kitchen
table. With the exception of wide slits in the old pallet, the table
has met all his needs. One side of the weathered gray slats was
wired to two pine trees and the opposite side was supported by two
tree branches. A great deal of time and care had gone into cutting
them from a cedar tree. Then, he had decoratively debarked and
carved them to fit with the same large knife.

A new tarp, which he assumed was trash, was recently stretched through the trees to cover his prized possessions, mostly consisting of his bedding. No one dared to tell him that Alexander gave instructions to make sure he discovered the purposefully abandoned roof for his home.

Several mirrors from old cars and broken dressers are strategically placed throughout his home. Each one is positioned in its unique angle, but when observed from different places in his home, each provides the same reflection; the cliff line behind his camp. Flopping down into his chair with the sketch pad, he glances nonchalantly at the largest mirror before him. Reflected over the hilt of his knife he confirms the presence of the Nephilim standing guard over his estate. He glances from the corner of his eye for he cannot...he must not...let the hellish creature know he is aware of his existence. For many months, he has monitored the ever present sentinels assigned to spy upon him.

Grabbing the pen viciously with his fist, he begins writing like a child who is having the first thrilling experience of creative expression. One in which, artistically, various colors of crayons are smeared on bedroom walls.

Today, he surmises, no new drawing will be added to his collection displayed on the tree limbs within his home. The collected works had no need of being secured by an over abundant use of wire. He snapped small limbs from the trees which left protruding stubs; and upon the stubs, he punched his paper collection. When the wind took them away and displayed them across the mountain side, he easily replaced them with new ones.

But today, he is the poet and thus begins his work of prose.

As the World Sleeps

MY GOD! Why hast thou forsaken me?
My feet do set to flight in the darkening hour,
I am soaked with the rain, sweat of flight and tears of despair!
My soul has descended to the rim of the pit, and I am alone,
Forsaken by friends and it is here I retire.

About me, the world races with dreams of tomorrow,
They seek fortunes and pleasures which bring me only sorrow.
The thunder is as loud as many waters,
And the lightning illumes my essences.
But where are you, oh my love? I do not feel your presences.

It's my love promising a door of refuge **WILL** always be opened,
But where dost thy dwell tonight when I **BE** sweat soakened?
In the dreaded heat of my never ending fight,
I feel the breath and smell the stench of the Dragon,
Your comforting voice I cannot hear and thus, I am saddened.

My eyes dull from the bright orb hanging in the sky,
Then darkness returns, like untrue love, and voices its lie.
My God!
Why hast thou brought me here to view such destruction?
Is there no one with whom I can share this bitter desolation?

There's no one with whom I can share the sorrow of my soul.
There's no one who will extend to me an offer of console.
There is no one.
No, there is no one in whom I can place my faith.
If there is, I will lay my armor down to feel their sweet embrace.

"My strength is dry as potsherd; my tongue cleaveth to my jaws;
And thou hast brought me into the dust of death."
My flesh is numb from a world of deceitful laws!
My bowels are poured out before me,
Who will? Nay, I cry...Who helping reach I will see?

If the world lies sleeping, I must reach out to you.
It is you only to whom I speak words that are true.
My head now doth clear, my ear doth hear
And my eye doth see!
And I know you have not forsaken, nor departed from me.

May I be **VICTORIOUS THIS NIGHT** with a clear mind,
For in such, I will declare thy name unto all of my kind.

Dan shoves the pad beneath the old cushion in his chair as he stands and stretches his arms to the darkening sky. Yet a full moon promises him that the darkness will be abated even after the setting sun. He knows the never ending battle raging between the two celestial orbs is soon to be won by the lesser. It will defeat the glowing sun, push it beneath the western horizon and celebrate by shining its glorious rays of victory upon the creatures of the night. He is not ignorant of another battle that is near to unfolding in the little town below his camp. Visions in his mind are crystallizing with the conception of his part in it; nevertheless, for the time he must sandwich them with foolish thoughts and verbiage. It was a thought pattern that prevented Vampires from reading his thoughts and had been taught to him by his ancestors.

Dan's Chinese ancestors had been employed to help construct the earliest railroads across the country. Eager to work their way westward in hopes of beginning new lives as free men, they soon discovered they were mere slaves to the railroad companies. When threatened with death because of sickness, which prevented them from carrying out their excessive labor, his grandparents escaped in the night heading north into the deserts of Nevada.

The next day, a couple of men rode out to bring them back to be hanged. Those men never returned. They were slain with a strange metallic staff Dan's great grandfather, Wu, had found in a burial cave; a cave also containing giant skeletons. The story passed down to him explained the skeletons to be nearly twice the size of human remains. After securing the safety of his family, Wu took the horses and rifles of the slain men and journeyed deeper into the wastelands. The family laboriously worked their way northwest across the mountains into northern California. The legend says that before Wu left, he returned the metal staff to its rightful owners to show his respect and gratitude.

It was his search for the cave and the strange staff that had brought Dan into the area years ago. Under the pretense of a prospector in search of silver and gold, he spent years searching for the cave. He was convinced the staff had been left there by aliens. Although he did not find it, the bloody vampires dwelling in the region had discovered a sword. A sword he felt had been labeled a staff by his ancestors.

"In time," he declares with no concern of the Nephilim sentinel behind him, "It will be rightfully mine."

Casting his eyes into a smaller mirror, he notices the Nephilim on the ledge is standing.

"Uh oh," he whispers. "I've really goofed up now!"

He dares to glare more closely at the one he knows is called Giles. To his amazement, Giles stands like a vulture glaring over Dan's head into the valley. Casting caution to the wind, Dan the Man whistles a tune unrecognizable by human ears, and Nephilim, and cries out loudly, "My sweet Rachel, where are you?"

With the distraction, he cocks his head to the right. A posture from which he feels he can observe Giles without being detected. Peeping into the canyon from the corner of his eyes, his heart jumps within his chest from shock for he marks two women and a man racing up the side of the mountain…toward his camp. Within minutes they will top the first butte of the mountain where he lives. Thereupon, and adjacent to his camp, lies the graveyard belonging to the people of the town. Dan overcomes his bewilderment knowing he must warn the trio of the demon that awaits them above his camp.

"But how am I going to achieve that?" he whispers. Nevertheless, he does not cease from the foolish tunes of his whistling.

Chapter 50

After Three, There is Four

"Though thou shouldest bray a fool in a mortar
among wheat with a pestle, yet will not his
foolishness depart from him."
Proverbs 27:22

"Hurry Rosie, we need to get started. Antonio is waiting for us!"

The widow replaces the sword in its black scabbard before answering with a question of her own. "What's the plan, Kara?"

"Rosie, there are three people in this town whose thoughts cannot be read by the Nephilim. That includes you, Antonio and a Chinese vagabond living near the top of the opposite mountain named Dan. Although they have different plans for each of you, the Nephilim intend to bring the three of you together...tonight, after the sun goes down! I think the three of you, and I, must come together before it gets dark to see if we can come up with a plan of our own to thwart their efforts, if possible!"

"You do know there's very little daylight left since we've spent most the afternoon here in your Dad's study? And Kara, I have to get out of these skimpy jogging clothes if you're planning on taking off up the other mountain side."

"That's exactly what I'm planning Rosie! Dad's at the Casino. He has three clan members with him: Philip, Dormin and Yegor. They will meet with all Banah in the valley shortly, along with a handful of humans. I'm supposed to be there so we must get to the top of the mountain before they become suspicious."

Kara dresses quickly with clothes she previously stashed in her father's desk. She leaves Alexander's Mastiffs inside his study as the two of them rush through the front door headed for the gates of the main entry. The Banah marvels at Rosie's ability to keep up with the grueling pace she has established for it is more than twice the speed recorded by any human. Onward they rush to a destiny that neither of them know the outcome to be. Through the gates they race, across the graveled road and down the slope of the rocky terrain of the mountain side toward Copper Town.

Within moments, they reach the base of the mountain. At that point, Rosie and Kara begin a slow, methodical jog through the south side of town – the residential area. Like two humans out on a pleasure run, they smile and wave at people they see along the way. However, once they get to Main Street, they observe people's reactions to be different. All of the stores along the street are owned by Nephilim and operated by their Banah offspring, or human employees who are loyal to the Shachar. Several of them quickly disappear into the shops casting a warning to both women that their arrival at Rosie's home may not be unannounced.

Neither of them knows what has given them away. Perhaps it was the swords swung over their backs or a warning sent from Alexander. Kara and Rosie look at each other with smiles acknowledging that it is time to throw caution to the wind and run. Immediately, they resume the grueling pace they had begun.

Within seconds, they both mount the stairs of the parsonage. After Kara turns toward the Rock and motions for Antonio to join them, she follows Rosie into the bedroom of the parsonage. The door is left open to allow the Hispanic gardener to enter upon arrival.

For the first time since leaving Kara's home, the widow feels like the skin of her legs are on fire. With her hands, she wipes away small streams of oozing blood caused by thick briars and thistles growing along the mountain side. She knows the answer but jokingly asks, "Is the terrain the same up the other side of the mountain?"

Kara gives her an affirmative nod, refusing to look away from Rosie as she slips from her sweaty clothing and tosses them to the nearest corner of the bedroom. Naked, she is unconcerned and unashamed as she faces Kara and observes that Antonio has joined them. No panties or bra had been employed in her run and none would be used now. Rosie walks to the closet and retrieves her leather riding pants. She firmly thrusts one leg at a time into the soft leather before yanking them to her waist. After snapping them, Rosie rushes past her two companions toward the tall chest of drawers. Freed from the restraints of clothing, her breasts bounce gently. Both Kara and Antonio examine them, for both are looking for the scars of the Yada that was placed between them by Slim and Alexander. The white orbs, although small, shine like new money against Rosie's glistening ebony skin.

Perhaps she has realized the intent of their scrutiny for Rosie rushes to cover her upper body with a dark tee shirt. Jerking a leather vest from the same drawer, she carries it with her to the bedside where she grabs her riding boots and plops down on the mattress to put them on. Rosie notices a thick pick handle grasped firmly in Antonio's hands. While sitting on the bed, she pulls on the heavy lugged riding boots and laces them firmly to provide extra support. She leaps to her feet and slips into the fringed black leather vest matching her pants. Rosie grabs the sheathed sword, which she had earlier tossed on the bed, and turns to inspect the troops.

She straightens, pushes her shoulders back and speaks.

"I'm almost ready!"

Antonio steps toward Rosie and pats her on the shoulder. It is an action meant to both comfort and encourage his new leader.

Allowing herself to look deep into his eyes, Rosie realizes this man believes in her cause and, if necessary, he is prepared to die defending her.

She glances at her reflection in the full length mirror and laughs. The black attire she is wearing makes her look more like an outlaw biker than a grieving widowed wife of a minister. Turning side ways to get a better look at her profile, she allows a few minutes of vanity, and wasted time to elapse before she secures the holstered sword to her belt. Again, she turns to the duo to speak, but this time she speaks with authority.

"Light is fading. Let's go!"

The three of them exit through the rear door. Kara descends the stair case with only two leaps and turns to wait on the others. To her surprise, she discovers Rosie standing beside her. Together they cast their eyes upward to observe the progress of their friend. Soft chuckles issue forth from both women as they watch Antonio slide down the rail. It is a ride that brings him to a jarring crash at their feet. Nevertheless, he jumps to his feet, dusts his pants with one hand and with the other he points his club to the top of the mountain they must quickly ascend.

Rosie and Kara begin the race. Across the parking lot they sprint. After passing the helipad, they cross the northern section of Loop Road and disappear into the cedars. From the cover of the thick vegetation, they turn to gauge the progress of the man who is following. Both women gasp with surprise for he is standing directly behind them. There is no time to speculate, or marvel at his achievement, for the sun is sinking fast into the desert. They must reach Dan's camp before the Nephilim arrive.

Upward they go with a pace equivalent to that which they began on the other side of the valley. In a short period of time, and with only a few hundred feet to go, Rosie fails to notice that Kara has stopped, frozen like an ice sculpture. As a result, she crashes into her back. It is a collision that sends them both toppling over the stony surface of the mountain side. But, both recover quickly leaping to their feet.

"Look," Kara points to the ledge of the high plateau which contained both, the town's only cemetery and the home of the Chinese man, Dan.

When Antonio joins them, the trio stands shoulder to shoulder as their faces contort with questioning puzzlement; for atop the rocky ledge above them stands Dan. He has watched them for some time and is pleased that he is finally the object of their attention.

Dan begins leaping up and down; first on one foot and then the other. His body slides along the cliff edge like a disco dancer while his arms reach openly toward the heavens. His mouth opens wide with mutterings they cannot discern. Dan's actions are unnerving even though they appear to be those of the mad man he is thought to be. And for a brief moment Rosie has no desire to continue upward to his place of residence. As the volume of his muttering increases, they hear the warning and watch as he points a jabbing finger upward to the rim rock behind him.

"Vampires riding in the sky…Vampires watching with an eye…Be careful Rachel! Be careful Rachel. Oh Rachel! Where are you? Come on home now. You hear me? But be careful, they really exist...vampires really do exist! You hear me Rachel?"

After singing the warning he hopes is understood, Dan continues the dance of foolishness.

This time, Antonio gives confidence to both women by patting their shoulders as he steps to the front, apparently to separate them from any danger above

"I'll take point!" He says before hurrying away.

The women hasten, but are unable to close the gap between them and the man leading the charge. Within seconds, he disappears from their view over the ledge. Unseen by the women, he is standing face to face, and within inches, of Dan the Man.

In a matter of seconds, Antonio is flanked by the Banah daughter of Alexander and the widowed wife of John Calvin. Both wield swords and are ready to battle against any force that might threaten Antonio. Rosie tosses her scabbard at the feet of Dan and instantly Kara's joins it with a loud rattle. The trio stands defiantly before the hermit and present an intimidating image of seasoned warriors who will not be defeated. With the coming darkness, it is an image that should intimidate all spectators; with one exception, Dan the Man.

Crowding together, the three who scaled the mountain discern, with appreciation, they have become four.

Chapter 51

Visions of Hunger

"Be thou diligent to know the state of thy flocks,
and look well to thy herds."
Proverbs 27:23

Hardened asphalt rushes upward and abrasively swipes the surface of his leather riding chaps. The contact presses deeper than he imagined. As a result, blood flows from the rip and covers his pants and chaps. He wonders if his decision to descend the four mile stretch into Copper Town from the crest of the Toiyabe mountain range with the engine off, and in neutral, might be the last resolution he ever makes.

He enters the sharp right-hand curve much too low and too fast. As a result, the inertia of his bike carries him within inches of the opposite shoulder. There, the graveled shoulders of the mountain road warn him if he runs off the pavement there will be no hope of keeping the bike erect. He fully understands if that happens, he will crash and at his current speed...he will be lucky to survive.

His heart pumps hard within his body as sweat begins to pour profusely from his forehead. Nevada law requires bikers to wear helmets but he foolishly strapped his to the top of his luggage. He desired to enjoy the rush of fresh air across his face and through his hair while he coasted down the mountain. Now, there is no time to second guess or change his plans. Coming out of the curve he appreciates the dearth of traffic on this lonely road for he is in the wrong lane. To further his dilemma, he observes there are no guardrails to protect him from the sheer rock cliff that drops into the canyon.

Years of experience, and perhaps luck, allow him to bring the bike into its rightful lane. Since applying brakes in the middle of a curve at high speeds is a formula for disaster, he breathes a sigh of relief for the short straightaway he sees ahead. Immediately he applies both brakes. Although unable to stop completely, he feels he can now negotiate the next curve in the opposite direction while staying in the right hand lane. All he can do is hope.

He eases off the brakes and leans the bike by pushing down on the handle grip. He has decided this time to enter on the upper side of the curve and work his way toward the inside. As his opposite knee slides along the pavement from the leaning cycle, again he is within inches of a graveled shoulder.

At least here he knows a mistake will send him crashing across the ditch and into the face of the mountain to his right and not over the cliff edge to his left. Ahead is another straightway before the road veers again to his right. This one permits adequate braking which allows him to negotiate the next curve and maintain his rightful place atop the asphalt. Successfully and safely completing this curve, he applies pressure to the brakes and comes to a stop at a scenic overlook to his left.

A safety barrier of cemented stone encompasses the overview and allows Dave to lean across it to observe the rocky surface below. He estimates the drop to be well over a hundred feet. Looking down at the sharp jagged rocks, he decides when the visit with his mother is over he'll ride back to Eureka and spend time with the waitress who angered him with her argument of their age difference.

"It'll take me two days at most to seduce that old floozy," he voices to the silence around him.

In the absences of human ears, Dave bravely voices his insolence.

"With a little persuasion, she'll see things my way or find herself at the bottom of this ravine."

He leans out again to view the rocky shelf below him and imagines her body lying bloody among the boulders.

"In fact," he declares, "that will be her fate regardless. And before that, I will do with her as I please. One way or the other, she will discover that age is not an issue with me!"

She would pay for all those degrading comments made to him. Comments like, "I'm old enough to be your mother!" And, "Did your Daddy let you borrow his big motorcycle?"

He gestures vulgarly to his surroundings and swears profusely, "she'll pay…I'll make her pay dearly."

He had witnessed several women plummeting to their death during the course of his life. And if all went well, he'd see more before he died.

Dave rests his elbows on the rock safety barrier to allow himself, once again, to pleasurably remember his first.

When he was sixteen, Dave spent the summer with his grandparents in Riley. His father's high school friend, George Landry, offered him part time work on his farm and Dave accepted. Although there was a generation of years separating them, they became close friends that summer. George owned a large sheep ranch in the area and was known throughout the region for his knowledge and expertise in herd management. He was also well known for his love and care for the flocks he owned. Along with raising sheep, George drove a supply truck for the local Farmer's Cooperative and would often take Dave along. One afternoon, George had to make an overnight trip to Columbus, Ohio to bring back a load of supplies. He invited young Dave to travel with him.

Before they got to Cincinnati, George received a phone call that his wife Patricia was entertaining another man in their home. The big rig turned and George headed home at breakneck speed. Not a word was spoken to Dave as George drove like a demon to arrive home shortly after midnight.

Upon arrival in Riley, he parked the semi at the Coop and retrieved his pickup. He told Dave he needed to stop at home for a second and then he would take him home. Dave remembers the darkness of the isolated farm house where his older friend slammed on his brakes and brought the truck to a sliding stop in his gravel drive. Another truck was parked among the trees adjacent to George's property. Although it seemed there might have been some hint of trying to hide it, it was visible enough to give a dash of boasting.

At that particular time, Dave knew very little about Patricia...that he liked. He sat watching as George retrieved a small revolver from the glove compartment of his truck before heading to the front door of his home; a home he had spent a lot of time and hard earned money on just to please Patricia.

Upon George's arrival at the front door, a light came on inside the foyer. Dave saw the door open and watched Patricia step outside the entry, completely naked, to hug her husband. George kissed his wife and tucked the pistol into his belt. She took her husband by the hand and the two of them disappeared into the house. When the door closed behind them, the lights were turned off and the interior of the house returned to darkness. Within seconds of the lights going out, a flash of yellow-orange light burst forth inside the living room and was quickly followed by a loud blast.

Dave slid down into the floorboard, but dared to look through the bottom of his open window. It seemed like an eternity passed before another man, half-dressed, ran from the front door carrying the remainder of his clothes. He leapt into his truck and sped away into the night. Knowing what had happened and filled with fear; Dave eased through the driver's door and crawled into the wooded area in front of George's home. He cautiously worked his way up the mountain side to watch the farm house. Within minutes, he saw police and emergency vehicles arriving at George's house. Long before the investigations were complete that night, Dave slowly negotiated the dark mountainous area to his grandparent's home.

The next day he told police that George did not tell him why they came back to Riley and after parking the semi, he dropped Dave off before going home.

According to Patricia, George was mortally wounded when his pistol went off when it was dropped on the floor. Police ruled it accidental, but Dave knew it was not. He never liked Patricia for she had flirted with him on a few occasions when George was not around. She was known by everyone in Riley, except her husband, as a woman who liked men and who spent a lot of time entertaining them when her husband was out of town. Dave knew the time she spent with the Deputy Sheriff, who sped away that night, served her well for it was he that conducted the investigation.

Within a week after George's death, Patricia called Dave to do some work for her. The flirtations began shortly after his arrival and Dave took advantage of them. He invited her for a midnight hike up the valley of the Big South Fork to a favorite swimming hole. She asked if they were going to skinny dip and Dave replied with a smile and a "yes".

The very same night, she picked Dave up on the isolated river road. He sneaked out and walked to their rendezvous. His secrecy was not due to an inability to secure permission from his grandparents, but was to protect them from what he planned. He could have no witnesses.

Patricia slid across the seat from the steering wheel to allow the young man to chauffeur her up the winding river road. Her move allowed just enough room for Dave to drive. As soon as the truck began to move, Patricia pushed her body against his and smothered his neck with a barrage of kisses. Her hands took the liberty of touching Dave in areas he had never been touched by a woman and before they arrived at the swimming hole, the truck veered into an old logging road. There, the front seat of George's truck became the bed of innocence lost.

Promises of a night filled with nothing but pleasure he had experienced with Patricia enticed him. And after fulfilling the promise of a "skinny-dip" in the chilling waters of the Big South Fork River, the seat of the truck, provided a place of pleasure again.

It was from the front seat of the truck that Dave formulated his plan. Jumping up quickly, he started dressing. He encouraged Patricia to do the same and told her of a high isolated overlook that few people were aware. At first she was hesitant, but with some comforting words of assurance, coupled with promises that their wild love making would continue atop the cliff, she agreed to the climb.

That night she proved to be more of an athlete than he had imagined. She needed no assistance from Dave in climbing to the summit. Atop the cliff, no time was wasted in his fulfillment of the pleasures he promised as the lust burning in his loins succumbed to the memory of what she had done to her husband.

He had kept that murder to himself, vowing he would be the avenger of George's death. And when the time came, he would be the one to punish her…and her lover.

With the beginning of new emotions growing within him, the tempo of their lustful deeds increased with proportional rhythm. It was a wild cadence which found her body thrashing hard into the rocky surface of the cliff. He envisioned the back side of her tanned body scratched bloody. Although he desired it, and labored to accomplish it, the skill of a sixteen year old boy was insufficient for the passion raging in the heart of an experienced woman.

He desired to hear her crying out with pain. Instead, he was confused from the moaning of a woman who begged for more of what he gave. Her legs encircled the narrow of his back as she came alive with excitement. The tidal motions of her body matched those of his, yet her waves began to crash on the rocky shores with greater force. He could not match the strength or powerfulness below him. Her finger nails raked his back and sank deep into forbidden areas of his body. Frustrated, he realized it was high time to rid himself of this murderous vixen.

The lack of experience can often be replaced by insatiable lust and so it was with Dave. Like a fireman fighting a wild fire with a large water hose, he fought until his back was covered with blood. The flow of his blood caused by her razor sharp nails was no less severe than hers…caused from the hard rocky surface underneath her. Nevertheless, when they collapsed totally exhausted, her sighs of contentment were not congruent with the growing hatred he had for her.

When he attempted to roll over to collapse on his back, she maintained her hold with both her arms and legs. Looking down at her smile, the rocky surface of their bed became a symbol of an altar of sacrifice which would finally grant him his revenge.

It was with a great deal of effort that Dave finally drew his bloody knees into a crawling position. This, in turn, allowed him to stand to his feet. Patricia never let go and as he stood on the rock, he also held her body tightly next to his.

With a quick and powerful move, Dave pried her legs loose forcing her to stand before him. When he yanked her arms free and pinned them behind her back, she purred like a kitten and laughed with expectation that their rest was going to be a short one. She moaned again looking lustfully into his eyes.

With his left hand, Dave tightened his grip on her hands while grabbing the narrow part of her back. The smile she gave him as an invitation to do as he pleased changed suddenly to panic when Dave lifted her above his head and tossed her over the ledge. He quickly moved to the edge for he wanted to see her free-fall of death. A scream barely escaped her lips as the flailing arms and legs smashed into the stones surrounding the swimming hole.

That was the first of many lives he had taken over the years. He had rid the world of several weak, inferior females; but that one was his most pleasurable. They say your first is always the most memorable. Dave had spent a lifetime seeking another one that would bring him as much pleasure as Patricia's; but as of now, none had given him the thrill of the first.

"Maybe," he declares retrieving his binoculars from the motorcycle, "the one who thinks she is old enough to be my momma will bring me the same ecstasy!"

He surrenders to his thoughts, *one thing is for sure, I hate that waitress as much as I hatred Patricia...if not more.*

"Time will tell," he whispers as he places the glasses to his eyes and leans over the rock barrier for a better look of the valley below.

Chapter 52

The Reunion

"For riches are not for ever: and doth the crown
endure to every generation?"
Proverbs 27:24

Swirling clouds of dust emerge from the canyon floor. They
appear to be on escape routes leading them upward into the sky.
Although clouding the vision of other drivers on the dusty road,
their attempts will be futile for soon they will settle, once again,
into the roadbed. Their efforts to break away are repeated
endlessly and hopelessly.

Through his field glasses, Dave sees the source of the
swirling clouds to be six vehicles traveling down Golden Canyon
Road in a tight bumper-to-bumper formation. Shifting his giant
binoculars to the right, he discovers that within minutes they will
leave the dusty canyon road to enter the asphalt streets of Copper
Town. Slowly, he scans the streets of the little town before
lowering his glasses atop the stone wall surrounding the scenic pull
over. With his eyes alone, he studies the winding road below him.
To his right, and lower than his observation point, a dog-leg curve
brings the highway beneath the overlook. Further to his left, the

road conquers the mountain with its last sharp turn before traversing westward through the town.

Viewed from the opposite mountain top, across Golden Canyon, Highway 50 looks like a large snake curled along the rocks and vegetation of the slope. Leaning out over the thick barrier, Dave correctly evaluates this section of the highway as the most dangerous in the state of Nevada.

The curve to his right is the one he is most interested in. Thus, he retrieves his glasses for further study. He zooms into the wooded area beyond the switch back and hoots with pleasure from his discovery. A topographical map revealed a westward ridge above the city, but he realizes it will be easier to negotiate than what he originally suspected for the pines are scarce having little under growth at this altitude. He needs to trek only a quarter of a mile along the ridge to arrive above a larger bench. The map labeled that large flat as the site of the town's only cemetery. If all goes as planned, he will hide his bike in the wooded area on the first ridge. Then he will ease down the mountain into Copper Town to begin the search for his mother.

Dave continues grinning as he quickens his pace back his cycle. He swings the glasses over his head allowing them to rest on his chest. Again, he elects not to start the engine. Swinging his leg across the seat, he pushes the bike atop the asphalt and relaxes as it resumes its coast down the mountain.

The bike rolls with ease; only a squeak of an unoiled section can be heard. Entering the curve, he softly taps the rear and front brakes while looking for a clear passage off the road. The twisting and turning of the handlebars steer his bike through the trees to a lower elevation. From there, he pushes it nearly two hundred yards; confident that it is now completely hidden. No vehicle traveling along Highway 50 will be aware that it is tucked away on the ridge line. Dave lowers the kick stand and watches it sink slightly into the sand. But the ground is firm, rocky and level; thus, the bike's lean is very near its normal position.

Loosening the cords securing the swords to his saddle bags, he stands erect holding both of them tightly in his left hand. Quickly and silently he moves through the trees on a path that will lead him to the rim rock above the graveyard.

Dave eases toward the new strategic point from which he will plan his final approach into the city. When softly lifting a tree limb to ease under, he glimpses something he has never seen. His actions are identical to that of the audience in a horror movie; he jumps backward with genuine fear. His path of escape is blocked by a dead tree into which he crashes violently with his back. Pain shoots through his body and his head throbs from the whiplash it suffered on contact with the lifeless cedar.

Dave's body slides down the tree trunk where he collapses in a helpless ball. Looking up at the hideous creature before him, he realizes he is doomed for the large monster stands twice as tall as Dave.

With eyes not dimmed by darkness, the Nephilim had watched and waited for the biker as he innocently walked into the trap. His large hands extend toward Dave as he originally planned…to twist his head from his body. But his plans would have to wait for Alexander had summoned him. Yet, he decides to amuse himself with one threatening step of advancement. When he sees the human's arms rise in fear, he laughs, turns and takes flight to Copper Town. The Nephilim leader is not to be kept waiting.

It takes a few seconds for Rosie's son to regain his composure, but with only a few minutes of sunlight left, he finds strength to crawl to the ledge for a peep below.

Inching his way along the large stone for a position that will allow him to see the valley below, he continues to scan the heavens; expecting any moment to be snatched away by the return of the creature. Once at the edge, he slowly glances down into the camp. There he sees four humans: two men and two women.

The first man appears oriental and the other is certainly of Hispanic descent. When his eyes catch sight of the first woman, he cannot believe what he is seeing. She is a beautiful woman. Her long blond hair hangs loose and bounces on her shoulders. Dave strains to see more, but the other woman has stepped between them.

"Get out of the way," he whispers.

She does not hear, nor would she obey if she did. He has no choice but to see what this one looks like. With her back to him, her features are covered by her black leather clothing. Her long hair falls down her back. Dave watches as she points to the town below. But when she steps to the ledge, motioning for the others to join her to watch the decent of the Nephilim, Dave recognizes her.

He stands, waves his arms and lets out a loud yell.

Chapter 53

A Gathering on the Mountain

"The hay appeareth, and the tender grass sheweth
itself and herbs of the mountains are gathered."
Proverbs 27:25

Climbing over the lip of the plateau, Rosie finds herself in the
midst of a trio. She nearly collapses from hysteria at the sight of
Dan who is still performing his crazy dance. With a jerk of his
thumb, he gestures to some unseen danger that lies behind him.
When Rosie snickers, he stares her into silence with a glare that
could freeze rain; then continues with mutterings of vampires until
his visitors shift their focus from him to the rim rock behind his
camp.

Squinting, Rosie is the first to see the Nephilim standing on
the ledge; complete in his majestic created form is Giles. He
stands looking down at the four of them, well aware that Dave is
approaching from behind. Darkened eyes of the ancient beast glare
with hatred at Rosie's party before he turns and disappears.
Almost instantly, he returns to the ledge and leaps into the night to
take flight. A flight pattern that will take him directly to
Alexander's gathering forces behind the casino. As he sails over

their heads, he spits on Kara and curses her. They all hear the warning he issues.

"So, you have sworn allegiance with these humans? Then be prepared to die. I'll leave it to your father to deal with you."

A voice rings out from the cliff where Giles took flight.

"Hey Mom…it's me…David!"

Recognizing the voice, Rosie turns eagerly to locate her son as her heart pounds with gratitude that he has made it to Copper Town. When she manages to locate the source of the voice, she discovers Dave standing with two swords in his left hand. She gasps and feels the beating of her heart which pounds within her like a symphony of drums. Joy overtakes her; a joy from discovering he has made it here alive. She whispers a prayer of thanks and motions for David to join them.

The ravine offers no resistance to her son and Rosie watches as he negotiates obstacles that would have slowed most men. Within seconds the two of them celebrate with a firm embrace that has no signs of ending. However, Kara shortens their reunion with a sharp warning.

"Rosie, we don't have much time. We have to come up with a plan before they get here"

"Okay," she says. "This is my son David. David this is Kara. And over here is Antonio. He was a good friend of your dad's. I don't know who this other…eh, fellow is?"

Kara makes the introduction, "That's Dan."

Dave shakes hands with all of them, but he cannot take his eyes from Kara. Thoughts of this beautiful woman, and how he might get to know her, race through his mind. Then they blossom into fantasies too forbidden to reveal.

Dan interrupts, "We must get organized for that vampire will return with several others. Look, the sun is near relinquishing its grip of the night. See the tender grass and trees around us? They have existed in this barren environment by mutual support of their ecosystem. We, too, must collectively stand united against the swarm that will soon seek to devour us. Together, we will endure."

Rosie is surprised with the sudden coherency of the little man she assumed to be a lunatic, but her surprise wanes quickly when Kara speaks.

"The Nephilim will arrive first and surround us. Don't give in to the vain glory of their appearance for it's meant to inspire awe; thus confusing our ability to think clearly. Our best hope will be from understanding their method of fighting. Keep your mind on what they will do, not what you see. Don't let them create fear in you, for it is your fear they can use against you."

"Next to arrive will be human servants followed by Banah. If we remain calm and focused, the first offensive will come from the humans. If that is not successful, which it will not be, the Banah will come. Now listen closely. When the children of Nephilim come against us, they will weave in and out attacking from different locations. They will attack and retreat repeatedly.

That strategy is meant to divide and separate us. If you become separated from our group, they will all gang up on you. Afterwards, they will single out another. There may be only five of us, but we can form a tight circle. As the fight progresses, remember this, all of them cannot get to us at once. So stay together. When you see a Banah wounded, all of us must shift as a unit and collectively slay that one. We will use their strategy against them. Understand?"

Her companions nod and listen to her instructions. They know their lives depend on it.

"If the Banah are defeated, the Nephilim will come. Be alert for they will make it three dimensional. Their attacks can, and usually do, come from above. Be ready. They will use humans and Banah to determine if a Bachar is among us. They do not single out or weave in and out. They have no given method. Do you understand?"

The heads of her comrades nod once more in unison. But, it is Rosie who answers.

"I'm ready and eager to get this started!"

She looks at Dave and continues, "Tonight, we get revenge on the ones that killed your father!"

"I know Mom," he says as he hands the Zulu sword to the unarmed Dan. With the success he had with the Samurai, he decides to keep it.

"Rosie," Kara beckons. "You will lead us. Our best defense will be an unexpected offensive which we will launch the very moment they get here. Antonio and I will take your right flank. David, you and Dan will take the left."

Kara positions herself slightly to the right and behind her new leader. Although there is adequate spacing to allow each one to maneuver, the formation is tight. As Antonio takes a similar place to the right of Kara, Dan and David take up identical position to Rosie's left. The power of the formation overflows among them and the hope that this wedge will be successful is accepted by all.

They wait...and as the last light of day surrenders completely to the silvery light of the moon, they hear a loud roar like giant locusts. It becomes louder as it approaches from the valley below. The sound increases with such intensity it nearly burst their ears. Yet, it is not sound that will threaten the stances they swore to be immovable. To the contrary, it will be their first sight of the source of the approaching light from the valley below. The threat of its revelation causes the moon to shy away from its inability to over-power the glory of the advancing light.

Chapter 54

Into the Stones of the Dead

"The lambs are for thy clothing, and the goats are
the price of the field."
Proverbs 27:26

Involuntarily, leather wings spanning thirty feet gently fold closed,
behind Giles. His flight from the mountain top to the parking lot
of the Casino has been a short one. The magnificent beauty of the
Nephilim alighting from his flight is viewed by those gathered in
the parking lot. The soft touch of his right foot atop the pavement
is followed quickly by his left. Spectacularly, it seems as if he
simply walked out of the heavens. His pace is not impeded by the
transition from flight to stride and within a few steps he covers the
twenty feet separating him from the leader of Clan Shachar. He is
a leader who is easily recognizable for he stands head above all
other Nephilim. Respectfully, Giles tilts his head and gazes
upward into the ancient eyes of his leader.

"Kara has joined forces with the Maseth," he reports to
Alexander.

"In the end, she will do as she is told," softly answers
Alexander.

"Nevertheless, no one is to touch the women; they are mine to deal with as I please. Understand?"

Under the close scrutiny of Alexander, Giles acknowledges the wishes of his leader. Quickly and in unison, the entire assembly consents to the wish, and directive, issued by their leader. Each knows failure to comply will result in death.

Easing to the side of his commander, Dormin "The Rebel" boldly asks the question which eons of dedication and support afford him.

"Do you think there is a Bachar among them? They have three of the remaining swords forged by the Ancient One. The other clans are most concerned with this gathering, Alexander!"

"We will soon know," the leader begins. "This very night, we will know if there is one amongst them. I think there's only two we have to be concerned about. Rosie's son, Dave, is a vicious murderer. And being such, he cannot be Maseth. That leaves us with Dan and Antonio. Both have resisted all our attempts to read their thoughts, but I am convinced that Dan is a genuine idiot."

Alexander had kept both men around for some time to study them. Long hours were exhausted by the Nephilim to find thought patterns that could be channeled. Usually, those channels were spontaneously accessed, but with some individuals it was difficult. The Nephilim describe the process as a labyrinth of cognitive flowing energy. By focusing upon a particular person's thought energy; they only needed to decode one thought. From that one, they could program the mind's logistic central process. This cryptogram was different for all people but were all based on factors molding the mind during behavioral development. Once that pattern was deciphered, the pathway into that mind was easily obtained from that time onward.

With time, Alexander felt he could discover the thought pattern of Antonio and that Giles would successfully track those of Dan; even if he was insane. It had not happened; thus, the entire clan feared to threaten them in any manner. Tonight, they would use their pawns to draw out any Bachar that might be among them. Their ultimate goal was to retrieve the last two swords that they might be forged into one.

"Okay, let's prepare to enter the stone shadows...shadows of the dead," commanded Alexander.

Effortlessly, his fluttering wings lift him swiftly into the night. His flight ascending to the town's graveyard provides the lead for his small army. Shachar's remaining members join him and within seconds, their formation is established high above and beyond the parking lot. Below the leader, the other four Nephilim form a diamond shape configuration. A position directly below Alexander is filled by his faithful and personal defender Dormin. Yegor follows a hundred feet behind Dormin. Between the two of them and equally spaced to the left and right, Philip and Giles soar like wingmen.

Consumed with hatred, Yegor endorses the destruction of all they will battle, including Alexander's daughter. His loathing is kindled from the beheadings of clan members Pavel and Vadis. The death of Pavel was avenged by his daughter Hunter when she single handedly defeated John Calvin who many thought was Bachar. Unfortunately, she was butchered by the preacher's son, David. Tonight, he swears to personally get even since Alexander promised David to him. He spits to the earth swearing once more that the death of Rosie's son will be slow and painful.

In the midst of flight, Yegor shakes his fists at the approaching rim rock before surrendering his disgust for ecstasy thinking that tonight he will taste human blood once again. He groans with incomprehensible utterings; excited that Antonio, too, will die. He assumed his slaying of Vadis had gone undetected by Shachar, but it had not! Bachar, or not Bachar, Yegor was willing to die to avenge the death of a fellow Nephilim.

As the formation nears the top of the ridge, Alexander rises upward to the center of the diamond shape below him. The Nephilim flight formation has become a prism similar to a pyramid. Prior to its revelation to the group in the graveyard, lightning surges throughout the cloudless sky. Every single bolt streams toward the pyramid providing it with energy unknown to mankind. Reaching the prism, the bolts are transformed into flashes of pure energy.

Four of them run lengthwise from Alexander downward to the four Nephilim located at the corners of the prism's base. Upon contact with the four, they explode like fireworks in the sky and continue outward to the other Nephilim along the base. There they remain as four strands of energy lacing the four Nephilim below together with their leader above.

Four more bolts of lightning-like energy join the four below, one to another. The result is a flaming pyramid skewed in its geometric manifestation. Brightly it shines, illuminating the night beyond the brightness of the moon. Like floodlights in a large football arena, the prism of energy will supply lighting necessary for the slaughter of the sheep, and the goats, waiting among the stone shadows.

When all lines are connected, each Nephilim glows similar to an electrical sphere. Below them, the army of twenty humans and ten Banah walk in a light brighter than day. They will need this light to defeat the enemy of Clan Shachar. Slowly and purposefully Alexander leads the army upward. He desires no surprise of attack. He will ascend with pride; fully in the glory of the Nephilim he was created to be.

Chapter 55

Food from a Maiden

"And thou shalt have goats' milk enough for thy food, for the food of thy household, and for the maintenance for thy maidens."
Proverbs 27:27

Helplessly, Rosie endured confinement within her home and the boundaries of Copper Town. Tonight, the anguish of the two week imprisonment submits to the fear she forgot. Forgotten until now; yet, inch by inch Rosie cautiously eases to the crest of the rim rock. Trembling hands are white from the death grip upon her sword. Until now, her only purpose in life was to destroy the Nephilim Leader, Alexander Gionni.

Breathing deeply, as if it will be her last, she readies the blade above her head, daring a gaze into the canyon. Determination to discover the source of the approaching light eases her fear. But, Rosie's peep of courage profits nothing for horror overtakes her when she gazes into the flaming eyes of her sworn nemesis. His flight above the trees brings him within close proximity of the preacher's wife. As to be expected, her discovery of the light source causes her to quiver; she leaps backward in shock. The spectacular lightning flashes surging from Alexander to the other Nephilim is not the reason of her alarm. Her fear comes into existence from a glare into the cursed eyes of the Nephilim leader as he rises to within feet of her.

Alexander's flight up the mountain, although steady, was impeded by the humans; nevertheless, when Rosie defiantly stared into his eyes, he sounded the call of her discovery to his army. It was an ear-splitting screech which sent echoes throughout the canyon and chills of terror into those gathered atop the cliff.

Forgetting the pressing wedge of companionship behind her, Rosie turns to escape. The collision with the wedge sends her bouncing backward in a course that would have carried her over the edge. However, Kara's quick reflexes enable her to grab Rosie's arm and easily pull her to safety. Kara's rescue is rewarded with an unexpected act of desertion as Rosie abandons the wedge and flees to safety at the base of the cliff behind them. But, somewhere in her defecting flight, she realizes the error of her deed and turns shamefully to face her companions. Once again her thoughts are overwhelmingly clear with the objective of her determination. If the vision of the approaching threat had momentarily frightened her, it now strengthened her; she will slay Alexander.

Serenely, she regains her composure and assumes the duties of her new command. The toes of her boots dig into the rocky ground; unruffled, she stares at the bright lights beyond her startled companions.

"Quick," she snaps, "back to the center of the graveyard."

Excitement overtakes her as she rushes past them to take up a new position. Turning to watch, she is amazed at the quickness of their response. They arrive within seconds. Their obedience reconfirms their allegiance as an increased potency of their resolve is displayed by their facial expression. None had viewed the canyon except Rosie; thus, no one knew what to expect. Nevertheless, they stand defiantly filled with trepidation of the unexpected.

Mixed emotions stir within Kara. She wonders if Rosie can be trusted. The Nephilim's attack will attempt to separate their enemies' leader from the troops.

Briefly, she glances at Rosie and wonders, *if they can send her running with only a display of supernatural powers, what will she do when the fighting begins? When we took our position in the graveyard, she deserted us again. Does she not know we must always move as a unit?*

Rosie glances at Kara and as their eyes connect, she detects the Banah's disappointment. She turns to face the impending battle and pledges her renewed devotion to their cause.

"Kara, I'm truly sorry. It won't happen again, I swear by the heavens above. We are in this together…until the end."

Determined once again, Rosie reaffirms her footing with the toes of her boots. Barely is the fighting formation of their wedge completed before a large globe of light rises from the valley floor and appears before them. With predetermined purpose it rises high over their heads in route to the cliff line; to the rear of their wedge. Looking into the fiery ball of energy, Rosie again identifies the Nephilim she knows as Alexander.

Four lines of energy flow from the leader over the shelf of the mountain like tow lines attached to something unseen in the depths of a darkened sea below. Alertness overtakes Rosie who realizes she cannot stand gazing into the sky. She snaps her head frontward again to see what the ends of these blazing lines might drag from the depths of the canyon. The ends of each rise above the wedge to reveal the four remaining members of Shachar. Their fiery presence is high above the wedge; yet it seems to form a boundary that Rosie and her friends will find impenetrable. Electrifying energy attaches them to their leader before springing forth to the others. The result is an emerging prism of pure energy that is near blinding to humans. It lights the marble stones so brightly, they seem to be part of the source of light.

As the Nephilim move, the bolts move like rubber bands stretching from one to the other; yet never breaking. The loud warning sound has not ceased since its inception.

Kara barks a warning as if she is now in command. "The sound is from the humming of the Nephilim. It is meant to distract you. Don't lose concentration. If we stand firm, it will fade away."

The last three orbs seem to form the point of an arrow beyond the cliff line. They provide light necessary for the humans to climb the rugged rim rock. Although Alexander ascends several hundred feet his ever faithful Dormin is positioned below him and closer to the wedge. Yet, the fiery lines of energy are not broken nor consumed. As the last three Nephilim resume their approach toward Rosie and her companions, the army of humans and Banah began to spill over the ledge. With no hesitation, they form two lines parallel to the wedge. To Rosie's right, ten humans stand armed with automatic weapons. Behind them are five Banah armed with a variety of swords and pistols. To her left is an identical group. All have sworn to die this night, if needed, for the cause of their masters.

Unfortunately, the wedge did not take the Nephilim by surprise. Rosie's group is in a hopeless cross-fire.

Chapter 56

Food from a Maiden - Part 2

"And thou shalt have goats' milk enough for thy food, for the food of thy household, and for the maintenance for thy maidens."
Proverbs 27:27

No explanation can be given for her actions. She does not know why she does it, she just swings the sword. Clearly, the familiar patterns of the numeral eight are formed before her. Created etchings upon the canvas of a cooling night sky, by the sharp blade, form arches of light very similar to those of the Nephilim. Refusing to fade under the canopy of the lighted prism, the soft orb of light surrounding Rosie chooses instead, to grow in intensity.

As if having a mind of its own, the sword of the Conquistador comes to a sudden stop above Rosie's head. Holding it firmly with both hands, she glares into the eyes of her enemy standing boldly before her. Suddenly, bolts of energy spark as bright as the sun. The bolts serve as a directive for the human slaves of the Nephilim to open fire on the wedge of Rosie's group.

All, including Alexander, are in awe from the unfolding spectacle. Each bullet fired, slows and falls to the earth within a few feet of the muzzles from which they escaped. Yet, the energy exerted from the discharged rounds is transformed into light which flows to the Conquistador. The sword's absorption of energy causes it to grow more intense with such brilliance it blinds the enemy opposing Rosie.

Another surge of energy flows along the prism delivering another command to Alexander's army. The humans drop their weapons and in unison, charge the wedge. Each gives a loud interpretation of a victory shout, for each believes their Nephilim masters will bring them victory.

Following Rosie's lead by readying their swords above their heads, the wedge awaits the onslaught. All, with the exception of Alexander, fail to see that the Zulu sword above Dan's head is glowing with a radiant light which is identical to the Conquistador.

"Dave, Antonio! Turn and guard the rear, but keep the wedge tight," shouts Kara when she observes the humans circling them.

Dave and Antonio turn quickly and close the gap to the rear of their wedge. Without hesitation, the first wave of attack comes against the wedge. They have replaced their discarded firearms with several different weapons including clubs, steel pipes, knives and swords. Each member of the wedge takes a few steps forward to allow adequate spacing to swing their weapons. Their preparation is revealed quickly when, with one swing, Rosie watches two men fall to the ground. Blood spews as they die helplessly on the earth. A third one dies when he makes contact with the lighted aura encompassing her body.

Kara steps forth with a spearing thrust of the Bonaparte into the chest of man she has known all her life. Unemotionally, she withdraws the blade and returns to the wedge while dropping two more men to the ground...headless.

Dan moves like the madman he is thought to be. Although he is not in tune, he sings a song he composed years ago. Moans of dying men around him seem to be more from the agony of his lyrical interpretation than from their deadly wounds. Nevertheless, he steps forth with three hasty swings of the Zulu that appear as one; three men fall to the ground. He dances on one foot while spinning in a circle. After closing his section of the wedge, he continues to sing, still out of tune, while hopping from one foot to the other. Within the wedge, his spear-like sword swirls to make geometric designs like Rosie's. The death of three from his blade is doubled to six when three more come into contact with the orb of light glowing around him. Dan kicks and shoves in an effort to clear the bodies piling up around him.

Slowly and like a ballet dancer, Dave extends his arm toward the first man charging him. His extension is increased by the Samurai he holds securely in his hand. The blade, reflecting eerie flickers of unnatural lighting, lashes out and returns with smears of blood from the stomach of the man it opened. Laughter escapes his lips as Dave steps back into the wedge.

He yells to his mother, "This may be easier than we thought, Mom!"

Unfortunately, he is unaware that Clan Shachar is analyzing each member of the wedge; an analysis which will assist them in their final attack.

Dave mimics Dan's dancing. With a leap, he moves too far beyond the wedge to claim the head of a second man before dropping to one knee to bury the Masamune sword to its hilt through the chest of a third. Surprisingly, the man reaches up with both hands and grabs the hilt of Dave's sword. Unexplainably, he refuses to allow the sword to be withdrawn from his body. Rosie's son simply laughs from the fact he no longer has to cloak his abnormal strength. He stands while lifting the man from the ground with the sword. Joyful visions flood his mind as he yearns to walk to the ledge and shake his blade free from this weakling of a man.

Although he does not comply with desires to look into the eyes of a human falling to death, he is distracted by the evil imagery. As a result, he fails to see a Banah sweep in from his right with a short sword, but he feels the sharp point when it punctures his body between his shoulders. Rosie's son collapses from shock when he sees the sharp point extruding six inches from his chest. Pain he never experienced surges through his body. Dave knows the blade missed his heart; yet, he knows he is mortally wounded. With the last efforts of his remaining strength, he manages to withdraw his Samurai. The blade in his chest has likewise disappeared. With extreme difficulty, he sits down and leans against the bodies of the men he has slain. He holds the sword in hopes of taking the life of the one that has taken his.

During his celebration of superiority, he was unaware the Nephilim had identified him as the weak link and sent Giles son, Illarion, to wound him. Illarion retreats to safety with the Banah and mocks Dave. His revenge is sweet for Rosti was his best friend and Len was his lover.

Antonio has no weapon other than the club. He is not ill equipped. Like a baseball player swinging a bat, he bashes the skull of the first man to arrive at his position. Switching his grip, he lowers his club with a downward stroke, twice in quick succession, shattering the skulls of two more. Tragically, his momentum carries him beyond the protective formation of the wedge away from Kara. Even though he has entered the ranks of the Banah, he splinters the skull of another man charging toward the daughter of Alexander.

Rosie watches as the Banah begin to circle her group. Two humans retreating with fear to the cliff ledge are beheaded by the Banah before they can make their escape. In less than a minute, her wedge has withstood the first wave of the Nephilim attack.

Outside the circle, Kara is outflanked by two of her kind. One of them is careless by forgetting Kara's life is to be determined by Alexander. He curses while rushing madly to embrace her in a bear hug; a hug in which he intends to crush her lungs. He never sees the quick flash of the Bonaparte blade cutting deep across the soft membrane of his throat. Instead of Kara's body, it is his he grabs in a futile attempt to stop the spasmodic spurting of his blood.

On the other side of the wedge, a hybrid sacrifices his life with a savage tackling of Dan. His contact with the arches of light rips him into as many pieces, but he succeeds in toppling the little man. The Zulu sword is dislodged and sails through the air. Unseen by Rosie, it falls close behind her. Dan rolls head-over-heels on the ground and comes to rest near Dave. His body aches from the viciousness of the blow and he shakes his head in an attempt to clear invisible cob webs from his head. The fading of the webs is replaced by the vision of two children of the Nephilim moving in to finish him.

"Here," whispers Dave with blood oozing from his lips! "Take this, I won't need it anymore."

Dan turns to see Dave holding the Masamune by its sharp blade. His foresight in handing the hilt to Dan will be advantageous. Knowing there is no time for conversation, Dan grabs the sword. He yanks it free quickly and as a result, blood pours from the hands of Rosie's son; his fingers are near severed.

Dan's actions are continuous. Leaping to his feet, he manages to side step the first Banah raging in like a mad bull. With a determined step toward the second Banah and a lightning quick flick of his wrist, he swings with all his strength. As a result, in the place where one Banah had charged, two halves lay in a pool of blood.

Quickly with mad slashes, Dan turns to face the first one, who has recovered from the failure of his first charge. The little man's precision swings whittle the second Banah into as many pieces as the first. Wisely, he refuses to celebrate his conquest and works his sword madly in an effort to reposition himself in the crumbling wedge. Dan does not see the brilliant yellow glow of his new sword, nor would he understand if he did. But with trepidation, the Nephilim know. The yellow arches glowing from the Masamune are brighter than the lights emitting from the prism. Genuine fear strikes the hearts of the Nephilim.

For the first time since their creation, Clan Shachar is engaged in mortal combat…with a Bachar empowered with his sword.

Chapter 57

Food from a Maiden-Part 3

"And thou shalt have goats' milk enough for thy
food, for the food of thy household, and for the
maintenance for thy maidens."
Proverbs 27:27

Serenity embraces the little wedge as a result of their
victory over the humans. Fresh assurance grows within as they
look for solid footing among the bloody bodies scattered around
their formation. Each member understands there is no time for
gloating or celebrating. Instead, they prepare to face the second
barrage of a new challenge. Although they face half the number of
Banah as they did humans, this battle will be more intense and
much more difficult. Their defensive is further impeded by the
corpses hindering them from obtaining firm footing.

Rosie realizes she is the focus of the attack when she sees a
Banah racing toward her with incredible speed. Unknown to her,
his charge is reckless for he has replaced vigilance with a thirst for
fame and fortune. He is determined to be the one that will pin her
helplessly to the ground before surrendering her to the pleasure of

Alexander. After watching Rosie's successful deployment of her sword during the human onslaught, two others follow more cautiously. Yet all have the same objective. Their desire to please the Nephilim is secondary to their dreams of wealth and power within the Nephilim Empire.

With her foot planted firmly atop a bloody human corpse, Rosie plunges forward with the fiery Conquistador. The sword sinks deep into the chest of the careless attacker; yet the drive of his charge sends Rosie backward causing her to topple to the ground were she is pinned by the body of the Banah she has just killed. She discovers that she is unable to overturn the corpse to withdraw her sword. Realizing Rosie's dilemma has left her unarmed, the other two Banah throw caution to the wind and charge forth with the same foolishness of their fallen companion.

Fumbling among bloody bodies and the rocky ground Rosie struggles desperately to regain her footing. Her fingers search for her father's pistol which she does not have. Instead, the smooth round shaft of an unfamiliar object is tightly grasped with her fist. The feelings of despair and hopelessness evaporate and are replaced with an exhilarating gust of energy; strength she has never known. Her supremacy is supplied by her clutch of the Zulu sword.

Rosie's reactions are instinctive. She looks at the body of a second dead Banah she unknowingly sliced in half with her new weapon. The sword is radiating with the same golden brilliance as the one held by Dan. The third Banah is shredded into pieces and sizzles from his contact with the rays of light surrounding Rosie's body. As the Zulu sword shines with lively brilliance, the lights of the Nephilim flicker to a dull luster. Rosie's war scream surfaces with discovery of what she has become while the Nephilim moan with distress. In unison, misery engulfs them from the revelation that their Bachar is…a woman. Never has the Ancient One chosen a female to champion his call. Yet, there is no mistake that the blazing sword held courageously in her hand is that of their slayer.

Rosie rushes to the wedge to regain her position as the leader. She hacks the air with the sword and, unlike Dan, sees the change of coloration in the arches of her swings. The light from the Zulu radiates brighter than the sun.

Unknown to the wedge, the Nephilim have joined the Banah for the final stage of their offensive. As the lights of the prism vanish, Rosie observes Giles' movement of stealth towards Kara and yells out a warning. It is too late! Giles' swift rush through the midst of the wedge is successful for his six inch talons leave four deep gashes across her stomach. Sadly, her intestines are exposed. Her sparkling eyes are filled with tears as she sags to the ground. She grips her stomach tightly to prevent spillage of her organs and looks sadly at her new friend. When she swore her allegiance to Rosie, she did not know her end would come so quickly.

With eyes fading of life, she screams out a warning, "Rosie! Look out! Philip is coming after you!"

Although she has not fully apprehended the metamorphic changes taking place within her body, Rosie perceives motion hundreds of times slower than she was accustomed, except for her own. She soars high with a vault that takes her away from the wedge. Landing on one foot she spins in a wide circle with the Zulu blazing bright. The sharp blade of the female Bachar extends outward and passes through the flesh of the Nephilim known as Philip. Rosie's strike is delivered with such concentration that the contact sends her rolling head-over-heels. Springing to her feet as if her loss of balance was rehearsed, she prepares for Philip's opposition; there is none. She hears the groan of a dying Nephilim before she sees his head topple from his body. In the twinkling of an eye, his remains sizzle and explode into a rain of dust.

Kara's eyes sparkle with wonder as she lies dying. The sound of thunder about her has been swallowed by the stillness of the night. She, nor the remaining Nephilim, dare move. None, including their fearless leader, anticipated the state of affairs which were unfolding before their eyes. It was as if the Ancient of Days had pulled a sick joke on them. While looking for the man who would be their Bachar, none had suspected a woman would emerge. It had never been before. But now, beyond doubt, Clan Shachar was being destroyed by a woman with ebony skin. She was the female Alexander ironically called his "Shining Blackness."

After an eternity which lasted only seconds, Giles rushes toward Antonio determined the Nephilim's plan would not be

275

altered. They would separate and destroy the resistance one member at a time; always seeking first, the weakest. Giles underestimates the little man. Moving through the wedge on his second charge, he slashes at Antonio with the razor sharp talons which mortally wounded Alexander's daughter. Antonio drops to the ground between the legs of the angry Nephilim. Although immortal, with the exception of losing his head, the blow of Antonio's club upward into his testicles sends agonizing pain into the nervous system of his monstrous body. Giles grabs the private members of his body, with proportionally large hands, and drops to his knees.

For years, Kara suspected there was more to Antonio than the Nephilim believed. All along, she sensed a supernatural presence woven within the nature of this little Latino friend and patiently waited for the day in which it would surface. Understanding she is to be part of his manifestation, she takes a deep breath and yells to him.

"Antonio…look at your feet! It's the sword Rosie had! Grab it…quickly!"

Agonizing pain does not prevent Kara from smiling as she collapses to her back.

Like a gazelle, Antonio springs to the sword and sweeps it up with a firm grasp. The moment it touches his flesh, a golden orb of light envelopes him as the sword radiates vividly. Antonio rushes forward and with a quick leap, he effortlessly severs the head of Giles, still caressing his testicles; parts of his anatomy he

276

will use no more. Another Nephilim vanishes into the moonlit night as a sparkling transformation of matter returns to the dust of the earth.

Chapter 58

Food from a Maiden - Part 4

"And thou shalt have goats' milk enough for thy
food, for the food of thy household, and for the
maintenance for thy maidens."
Proverbs 27:27

Rosie, Dan and Antonio rush forward to form a shortened formation of the original wedge. The radiance of individual swords coming into the hands of the Bachar for which they had been forged is beyond human description. And as the three unite in close proximity, their luminosity is heightened to further levels of marvel. The spectacular demonstration of unleashed power has never been viewed by mankind, or Nephilim, since the foundation of the Earth. It was an ordination from the Ancient of Days to counter the Nephilim plan to merge their three remaining clans.

Majestically, three Bachar slowly and purposefully twirl their swords in circles of unison. Looks of confidence and assurance is discerned within the features of their faces. Facial features that should have warned Yegor to flee for his life are ignored from the anger boiling within him. Anger fueled from the loss of two more of his ancient clan members. Overwhelmed, thoughtlessly he rushes alone toward the inferno of the three Bachar. Rosie steps from the wedge to meet him. She portrays the image of a small kitten on an inevitable collision with the beast charging her; a beast nearly three times larger. If a long and enduring fight is anticipated by Alexander and Dormin, they will soon be stunned.

Rosie avoids the Nephilim's charge with a quick evasive move to her left. Her sword leaves a glowing trail of the route it took to remove Yegor's right leg at his knee. He stumbles and falls to his face among the growing pile of flesh and blood.

To those watching, it appears that Rosie is performing a contemporary dance. She bounces and whirls around Yegor. In addition, she jabs and slices at the body of the Nephilim with the Zulu in ritualistic exploits. But when she returns to face the fallen creature, his body crumbles to the grounds in severed pieces.

After the fireworks display of another vanquished Nephilim, she elects not to return to the wedge for her sword was ignited with the power of the Ancient of Days.

Rosie stands defiantly glaring at the darkened form standing on the rocky cliff she knows as Alexander. Below him, his personal champion Dormin is shocked.

Her eagerness to destroy the remaining members of Shachar is diverted by the vision of her son who lies dying near her feet. Totally engrossed in battle by her will to survive, she was unaware of his injury. Her heart is torn. She desires both; to rush to her son and comfort him in her arms as she did when he was a child and to finish the destruction of Shachar. Above her stands the monster which killed her husband and has claimed the life of her son. In the end, her love for David suppresses the hatred for Alexander.

Dan and Antonio are as anxious to finish this fight as Rosie, but both are supportive for the mother who will comfort her son in the last minutes of his life.

Telepathically, Alexander and Dormin argue.

I can take them Alexander. Let's not leave here tonight like cowards for our clan is all but gone. The Bachar cannot be a woman!

No, my old friend! Listen to me. Do as I say. Go down to the helicopter and we will fly to Reno. There, we will take the jet to New York and then to Spain. Here before us are the three remaining Bachar. They must be divided. Can you not see that Rosie is the Bachar of our clan? One of the other clans will have to slay her. I see clearly now that we can succeed if we fight the other clan's Bachar. Now go. I have one last thing to do here before I retrieve the other swords and join you.

The gathering in the graveyard is surprised and amazed at what appears to be the desertion of Dormin. One minute he stands before them with vicious eyes of hatred and the next...he is gone. Looking upward they see Alexander spread his wings and slowly ascend into the sky. He becomes silhouetted in the full moon before he, too, disappears into the canyon.

Kara begs, "Rosie, go now! Follow them into the canyon! You cannot let them get away to regroup. Please, I'm begging you. Go now!"

Something confirms Kara's plea is the right thing to do, but Rosie's love for her son cannot be denied. She kneels by his side and whispers words of love to a son she knows is dying.

Unknown, and unseen by them, Alexander took to his feet below the graveyard and worked his way back to Kara. He demands her mind through the channels of memory he long ago forged. There, for the first time, he expresses his love for her. At first she feels his words are not sincere, but she has long desired to hear the feelings he now shares. His hands slither through the thick vegetation near her crumpled body and tenderly rub her wounds. Kara is healed by the hands of a Nephilim Raphah. To her, it is an obvious display of the love he quietly expresses.

"My dear daughter, your scars I will leave as a reminder of your betrayal, but you will live. Remember, I will see you again and when I call you to assist me, you will do as I say. Do you understand?"

"Yes!" she says. Her answer is more from fear than obedience for her thoughts are not completely her own.

Alexander lingers to observe his nemesis in her final moments with her son. He wonders if she will forsake her faithfulness to the Ancient of Days and ask him to heal her son.

Chapter 59

The Final Victory

"O death, where is thy sting? O grave, where is
thy victory?"
1 Corinthians 15:55

"Davy, can you hear me?"

Rosie drops to her knees beside Dave and tenderly gathers his body in her arms. The act is accomplished with such gentleness that her comrades are reminded of a mother holding her newborn child for the first time. Regrettable, her expressions reveal the fact she knows her son is dying. She stares at his closed eyes as if she can rescue him from the eternity into which he is passing by her simple will. The sigh escaping from her lips establishes the fact she cannot, but her love remains unfading. Her voice quivers in privacy with a prayer none of her friends hear; she is rewarded with the answer to her supplication when Dave's eyes open for one last time.

As she rocks him in her arms, he focuses completely upon the face of his mother. His shallow breathing warns Rosie their time together will be brief, yet she whispers another prayer of thanks that she has be granted the opportunity to look one last time into his blue eyes.

For a moment, his mother comes close to rushing to the crest of the mountain side and calling for Alexander as she did the night she was attacked by the motorcycle gang. She, more than others, understood the supernatural healing powers of a Nephilim Raphah. The love she has for her son compels her to forsake the cause, surrender to the Nephilim leader and plead for Dave's healing. But her loyalty and commitment to the Ancient of Days provides her with the strength she needs. The reality of Alexander having her husband slain kindles the spark of faithfulness she maintains; she cries in destitution. The hatred growing in her heart for Alexander ebbs as she comforts her son with flooding tears that splatter on his face. Rosie wipes them away before she squeezes him tightly to her bosom.

"Dave," she begins to ask. "Have you made your peace with...."

"Mom," he interrupts before she can finish.

"You know more than anyone, I don't believe as you and Dad. I'm ready for whatever lies on the other side."

"Davy, my sweet Davy, I have known since you were a child that you would struggle with faith. Can you not just once believe and plead for mercy?"

"I believe mom, but it is not meant for me to be. I've lived a very evil life and if I were to survive this, I'd go on pursuing the same pleasures of this world. Can you not understand that?"

"Yes, I am afraid I understand more than I want."

"Mom...my superhuman abilities...do they come from the fact that I am the son of a Nephilim? Tell me truthfully, do I exist because you mated with one of them? I need to know before I die, so please don't lie to me."

Rosie shakes her head in denial, disappointment clearly displayed by her facial features.

"Davy, how can you ask that? I have known no man, other than your father. Where did you get such a ridiculous thought as that?"

Gasping for breath, several moments pass before Dave gathers his vanishing strength to answer. He is determined to complete this conversation before he passes.

"Hunter said I was her brother and that her father took you when you were younger. To me, mom, it explains the incredible strength and evil desires I have. Don't you think?"

"Dave," she continues, "these creatures and their offspring are liars. You cannot believe anything they say. As for your strength, it comes from the fact that I am the chosen Bachar of the Clan Shachar. Your strength was inherited from me, yet it springs from the omnipotence of the Ancient One."

Chapter 60

Last Words of Warning

"…then shall be brought to pass the saying that is
written, Death is swallowed up in victory."
1 Corinthians 15:54

Resurrected forms of light rapture among the stone shadows;
emerging like erupting geysers. Each one gloriously outshines
any, and all, other sources of illumination. Collectively, they cause
all but Rosie and David to cover their eyes with their hands.
Bewildered, David looks at his mother with confusion before they
both turn to watch the great event taking place among the marble
headstones.

At first the lights seem ghostly, but soon take on the form
of humans. All appear to recognize Rosie as being one of them.
Although, they must journey on, they know she has been chosen to
tarry a little longer. The female Bachar nods in reply and quickly
looks down at her son in hope that he too will join their ranks; he
does not.

With no further delay, the lights ascend skyward and
vanish. It is then that Rosie addresses her friends.

"Would you give me few moments to be alone with my son?" Rosie asks

The other two Bachar, move to the hillside to observe the lights of Copper Town. From there, they are unable to hear the conversation between Rosie and her son. However, hidden beyond his healed daughter, Alexander listens intently.

"Mom, I know what just transpired and I know why I was not part of it. But tell me, why were you left?"

"God has left me and the other two to finish the work he began in us. It will all come to pass Dave. And I promise you son, I will avenge your death!"

With those words she watches as her son exhales his last breath of life. His body rests calmly in her arms as she begins to rock. A song none of them know, but Alexander, melodiously flows into the night. A song of another day, another time and another country in which there will be no pain of death or sorrow. Her tears increase to the point that the salty taste seeps between her lips. When the song is completed, Rosie closes the eyes of her son affectionately with her fingers. Lifting her head to the heavens she pleads once more to a God she knows is listening.

With *amen*, she turns to watch Kara slowly standing to her feet completely healed, but it is not Kara she seeks to monitor. Unseen in the vegetation and darkness beyond his daughter, Alexander knows he is not visible. Yet, he is outraged as Rosie looks fiercely into his ancient eyes.

"I know you are there. The next time we meet, you will not take me by surprise. Go now and do that which you do quickly while I bury my son."

After a loud rush that sounds like thunder, Rosie stands with her son in her arms. She walks to the ledge where she joins the other Bachar. Together, they watch the leader of Clan Shachar glide into the gorge. Soon he will sit on the throne of his World Empire where he will enjoy peace for a little season. A season that will be short lived for this day he was unable to defeat three Warriors of the Sword. Someday, the three he left behind will stand before him…AGAIN!

"Help me bury my son," Rosie pleads. "And then we will begin the end of the Nephilim. They have walked among mankind since their creation, unbeknownst by most.

But one thing is for sure, the Nephilim know we are alive and for the first time in their existence, there is no doubt they will abide in fear…for their destruction is nigh."

From the Author

For many years I have been intrigued with "The Revelation of Saint John the Divine". I have discovered things that baffle the mind of men and confuse many theologians. My fictional story explains the fables of vampires as real interactions between men and Nephilim. Nephilim are ancient beings who have dwelt among humans since their creation. They have always desired dominion over mankind.

The Greek word *agorazo* means to purchase from the market place. In Scripture, that market place is Earth. The purchase encompasses the entire composition of man: body, soul and spirit. Thus, true redemption is completed only after the resurrection process. (See 1 Corinthians, chapter 15 and the teachings of Jesus in Luke 20: 27-38). Now, this is where it gets interesting. We suppose Scripture is for mankind and us alone; however, Revelation 5: 8-10 reads as follows:

*And when he had taken the book the four **beasts** and four and twenty elders fell down before the Lamb, having every one of them harps, and golden vials full of odours, which are the prayers of saints. And they sung a new song, saying, Thou are worthy to take the book, and to open the seals thereof: for thou wast slain, and hast **redeemed** us to God by thy blood out of every kindred, and tongue, and people, and nation; And hast made us unto our God kings and priests: and we shall reign on the **earth**.* (KJV, bold emphasis by the author).

Many Bible scholars agree that the twenty-four elders represent mankind but disagree as to what classes, or nationalities of men. I feel that nearly all overlook the beasts; or fail to see that they also are resurrected from the dead since they are redeemed. Angels cannot be redeemed for they do not die as they are created spiritual beings and have no physical bodies. Logically, these beasts could very well be in existence today. Could it be that we cannot see them because we are blinded to the spiritual realm which is beyond our own self-centered perception of reality?

288

Two classes of beasts are found in The Revelation. The first is interpreted as beast, or living creature, from the Greek word *zoon*. It means living thing, animal life, or living creature. They are not human! Yet, they sing the song of redemption.

The other class is *therion*. Interpreted in English as "beast" yet there is something different about them. The Greek word means a living creature that is venomous. Thus, as mankind, the beasts are both, fallen and redeemed.

Kenneth Davidson